AMILAH

Halima Hagi-Mohamed

For my family and friends

"And We will surely test you with something of fear and hunger and a loss of wealth and lives and fruits, but give good tidings to the patient" Quran 2:155

PREFACE

Throughout my short history of writing I always knew I wanted to write a book. I just couldn't figure out what it would be about. I was sold on the idea of fiction and I began from there. I had no name for my book then but wrote my stories anyway. All of the stories were about Somalis and covered issues like depression, love, relationships, and religion. I went back and forth between names for my book. Nothing seemed to stick. I quit writing it in 2014.

A year later, while scribbling my name over my diary something struck me. My name backwards seemed to spell out to something. Amilah. I looked it up and discovered that it meant '*hopeful*' in Arabic. This realization overwhelmed me. I grew obsessed with the idea of hope and the name Amilah itself. It became all I could ever think about. I decided this could be the name of my unfinished book. So I went on calling it that and telling anyone who was willing to listen.

In December of 2016 I was advised by my older sister Anisa to chase after my dream and finish writing my book. Her advice seemed to really hit me. With the promise of her full support and dedication I dove back into writing. A close friend of mine, Hodan also pushed me to fulfill my dream and gave me beautiful words of encouragement.

With the support of family and friends I went after my book. I gave it my full focus and attention this time around. I scrapped some stories that I didn't think were a fit and rewrote what I seemed to like. I honestly never knew revision could be such a pain. There were many times while writing this that I wanted to give up. I told myself it didn't matter and fed myself many excuses.

Thankfully I continued writing and pushed myself to go on further. I knew that this book was important outside of my own desire of fulfillment. The stories I wrote shed a light on darker issues facing my community and humanity as a whole. That meant something to me. Now here you have my finished work before you. I hope it captures your interest and causes you to reflect. Each story deals with battles many face in this life. The interpretation is solely your own.

I'd like you to know that Amilah isn't just a word for me. It's so much more than that. It was a motto that uplifted me throughout this writing process. There were many times I felt defeated. Rejection stared me in the face through countless emails from agents and my own demons. I had dark moments but I didn't let them stand in my way. Whatever it is that's forcing you to fight is important. You need to realize that now. Tackle it head on and don't give up. Keep hope alive and thrive.

Much love. - Halima

CONTENTS

AMILAH

I tore through my closet in search of things I needed to take. My eyes were blurred with tears and I could hardly tell my clothes apart. Everything seemed so disorganized and cluttered. I turned back to the door to make sure it was indeed locked. He could break through it at any point. I would be naive to think he wouldn't. My adrenaline was skyrocketing as tears streamed down my face. Over time I collected an abundance of painful memories because of him. I endured physical and emotional abuse and still stayed. For one reason or another, I never left.

I roughly wiped at my tears and tried to settle myself down. Khalid wouldn't come after me. The things that happened an hour ago cemented that. I took a deep breath and stood in front of our walk in closet. My eyes fixated onto Khalid's wardrobe. All of his shirts and suit coats were neatly organized and color coated. There wasn't a single item hanging unevenly from a rack nor a shirt that looked worn and wrinkled. I fought the urge to tear everything of his apart. When I reached out to grab one of his shirts, I noticed some lint on the shoulder of his coat. I was surprised he hadn't caught it before. Khalid was totally anal about his things and even admitted being so when we first met.

Aside from this flaw, I was convinced Khalid was my dream man. He was tall, handsome, accomplished and suave. Before I met him I completely gave up on the idea of love and marriage. I had just gotten out of a messy relationship of six years. I promised myself to never fall in love again and avoid men all together. I lost all hope of finding my Mr. Right.

Three months later I met him. By chance we both happened to be at one of the three weddings taking place that same night. His eyes lingered over me for an eternity before finally introducing himself. My

1

first impression of him was that he was incredibly charming and handsome. I was mesmerized as he spoke of his engineering job, passion for hiking, and growing book collection. The wedding went unnoticed by us as our conversation grew deeper into the night. Before leaving, Khalid asked me for my number, which I happily gave to him. We were completely inseparable from that point on. There wasn't a day that went by where we didn't phone or message each other. Our love had reached its peak and I was enjoying the impeccable view. Three weeks later, Khalid proposed. It was pretty fast but I was convinced he was the one, so there was no looking back. Deep down inside I imagined myself being his wife and mother to his kids. I was sold on the idea of our love and marriage. To be honest, Khalid had me at *salaam*.

After having the wedding of our dreams, surrounded by doting friends and family, we were living in bliss. I never remembered being so happy before. It wasn't very long into our honeymoon that I started noticing some things about my new husband that I didn't like. He had these overwhelming jealous and overprotective tendencies. I even began to start doubting myself with how obsessive he became. I didn't have very many male friends but with Khalid's paranoia I made sure to keep none.

At first I believed he would change and quit acting the way he was but I couldn't have been more wrong. Weeks later, Khalid made me give him my *Facebook* password. Both of us kept the same passwords on our phones, so I didn't think it was so big of a deal. Khalid explained that it would be a good idea in case either of us needed to get into each other's accounts. I thought it was a silly reason at first but went along with it anyway. Later, he decided he wanted to know all of my social network passwords. That's when I knew he didn't trust me. Even though it frustrated me, I let it go and told myself it wasn't anything to get worked up about.

I took a deep breath and looked through my things hanging in my side of the closet. That's when my eyes fell upon it. My navy blue pea coat. Two of the buttons were missing because of him. I remembered the day it happened like it was yesterday.

I had just gotten back from my friend Zahra's belated birthday dinner. A lot of my friends and even Zahra herself, were unable to meet on her actual birthday, so we planned for the following weekend. I made sure to clear it up with Khalid a whole four days before. He was always so uptight about those kinds of things. I had been married to him for six months and he still made it a point to know my every move.

That night, I stood outside of the door and dug through my purse for the key. I could've just knocked or rang the doorbell but I didn't want to wake Khalid. He could have been sleeping since it was almost one a.m. And it was Monday the next day so he'd have to wake up early in the morning for work. After a few more seconds of searching I found my key and put it through the door hole. Unsurprisingly, the house was utterly dark and I had to use the flashlight on my phone to make my way through. I was headed upstairs when I felt a gentle tug on my coat.

I jumped back frightened and dropped my bag in the process. There lounging on the sofa was Khalid, looking right at me. I sighed relieved and bent down to pick up my bag.

"Babe you scared me," I said a little out of breath. I assumed he'd be in bed by now.

He said nothing in response as I pulled my bag back over my shoulder.

"You didn't have to wait up for me," I told him, a little annoyed. I waited for him to say something but all he did was stare at me. I

3

thought it strange at first but knew he had his weird moments, so I didn't think much of it at the time.

"I'm going up to bed. I'm beat," I said, dragging my tired feet towards the stairs.

All of a sudden the lamp flickered on. I turned around to see Khalid sitting up, hands locked together, and glaring at me. Something in my heart grew heavy from his stare. It was like something just turned on in his eyes.

"You didn't even bother to call me and let me know where you were." He said livid. His eyes were narrowed and he looked to be wide awake now. So why was he being so quiet earlier I wondered.

"I told you I'd be going out tonight, remember?" I asked trying to spark his memory.

"Now you're lying to me," he muttered, lowering his eyes away from me. I watched in confusion as he shook his head.

I laughed. "No I'm not. I told you four whole days ago, remember? Zahra's birthday dinner at the *Cheesecake*. Why are you acting like you don't remember? God Khalid, it's late and I'm too tired for this."

I treaded off towards the stairs. I wouldn't entertain his bullshit all night. I was too exhausted to talk anymore. Just as I was going to take my first step upstairs my arm was tugged from behind.

Khalid exhaled. "Don't walk away while I'm talking to you."

"What the hell is your problem? That hurt," I complained, dropping my bag onto the steps. I held my arm close and gave him a dirty look.

4

"I don't care. Now tell me why you think it's okay for you to leave and not bother telling me where you go?" he barked, gripping the stair railing.

"I don't know if you forgot but I'm your husband. And you have to get *my* permission to leave the house and see whoever the hell it is you want. Just remember that."

I was in complete disbelief, with my arm still aching in pain. I looked at him expecting he'd come back to his senses and apologize for his brute behavior but that never happened.

"Next time you tell me ahead of time. Got that?" He spat as he pushed past me upstairs. I watched as he walked on ahead, unaffected by my pain and shock. My eyes grew wet and I wanted nothing more than to slap him across his stupid face.

"I don't have to tell you a thing. *Got that?* Just who do you think you are anyway?" I said breaking my silence. Almost instantly he stopped midway on the stairs and turned back around to face me. I was afraid but I had to stand my ground. I shivered as he took slow steps towards me and smiled. Then out of nowhere he grabbed a hold of me, and in the process tore two buttons from my pea coat. I cowered back in fear as he shook me over and over.

"Don't you ever talk to me like that again! Do you hear me?!" He shouted. It was almost two in the morning and he was hollering like a maniac. I prayed the neighbors wouldn't complain from all the noise.

Tears fell from my eyes when he let me go. I dropped to my knees and bawled into my hands, feeling powerless and small. I must have stayed there for over twenty minutes before I changed into my pjs' and curled up on the sofa. I didn't sleep that night. I was hurt but most of all surprised. Never would I have expected Khalid to be so rough with me. Little did I know at the time, it wouldn't end there. That night was like a gateway drug for Khalid. Abusing me became his regular poison.

****

I set my things on the ground and took one last look at the house I'd be leaving behind. I admired the expensive carpets imported from Dubai, and almond colored leather sofas. It was beautiful but not at the expense of my own safety and peace of mind. Khalid liked to believe he could buy me this kind of lifestyle in exchange for my happiness but he couldn't be more wrong.

I grabbed my bags and opened the front door. I would never come back here, not in a million years. I didn't care if Khalid dropped down on his knees and begged me. I wanted this place, this part of my life as far behind me as possible. It was time to turn a new leaf, alone. I shut the door behind me and quickly made my way to the car. I put my things beside me in the passenger seat and backed out of the driveway. He hadn't showed up yet, but I wasn't going to sit around waiting till he did. He was his worst right after something like this.

As I drove through the maze of suburbia I thought of my future. Where would life take me next? I had made the quick decision to stay with my friend Marwa but that couldn't be permanent. I'd have to find my own place and live on my own someday, even though the thought of that scared me to death. What if he found me? I'd be entirely alone with no one to protect me against him. My eyes filled back up with tears and I thought back to the last time he lashed out against me. He grew upset over the smallest things and always made sure he got the last word in.

Whenever I tried speaking up for myself he'd unleash his inner monster. His harsh words and cruel force were his weapons of choice. Khalid always made me feel so worthless. I hated looking at myself the next day in the mirror. It felt like the words "weak" and "pathetic" were scribbled all over my face. The emotional damage was much worse than the bruises he left on my body.

I was driving through the, *"Ashland District"* now. Khalid and I had come here for our first *Eid*. We had just got done eating brunch at the *Broken Yolk* and decided to do a little window shopping to kill time. Khalid was a little over dressed in his black suit and velvet tie but insisted he didn't want to go home and change. We were having a really great time and grabbed some frozen yoghurt too.

At one point I remember having to use the restroom. Khalid suggested I leave my bag with him and I did. When I came back I found him with my phone in his hand, scrolling away as if it were perfectly normal. He didn't even stop once he saw me. It was like he wanted me to know he didn't care or thought nothing of my privacy. There were a lot of people around so I just kept my cool and playfully snatched it from his hand.

He didn't seem to find that very funny. Khalid and I got quiet afterwards or at least that's what I remember. I knew why I was so uncomfortable and silent but couldn't understand why Khalid was. As soon as we headed back to the car the silence was broken.

"Do you have anything you need to tell me?" He asked, through gritted teeth.

I laughed and sort of shrugged. "What would that be?"

He got into the driver's seat and slammed the door shut. I remember feeling the hair on my arms rising. For as long as I could remember my intuition was never wrong. I watched in fear as he sighed and looked straight ahead. I shifted around in my seat and asked myself what it was that set him off.

Then out of nowhere he slammed his fists down on the opposite ends of the wheel. I shrunk into my seat and looked at him with a heart full of terror.

"Babe...wha-what's wrong?"I blurted naively.

He turned his head towards me and smiled. There was an icy look in his eyes.

"You're honestly scaring me. What is it?" I asked bewildered.

"You think you're so sneaky, don't you? What makes you think you can hide anything from me?"

I sat still as the air around seemed to suffocate me. I looked into his cold eyes and asked myself what in the world he could be referring to. What had I done so wrong this time?

"I saw your messages. You called me the big bad wolf, and why do you still have your ex's number saved? Are you keeping it for a rainy day?" He asked tilting his head as he said it.

I scoffed. "You're unbelievable. I can't....I just can't. What do you honestly expect me to say?"

"I expect you to say something. We're not leaving this parking lot until you do."

"Khalid, it's *Eid*. Can we just have a drama-free day for once? Seriously, I'm sick of this."

He flung his keys onto the dashboard. "I'm being completely serious too."

8

"So am I! I don't want to keep arguing with you! Why do y[c] need to find something to get pissed about?!" I huffed and pu[..] of breath.

Meanwhile, he was completely calm.

"You're full of shit. You're not the victim here Amilah. So stop acting like you are." He muttered.

I pulled out my phone and deleted my ex's number and waved it in front of his face.

"Happy?!" I cried out, close to tears. "God you're going to drive me insane Khalid."

"And how am I supposed to know if you don't already have it memorized?"

I laughed, tossing my head back like I just heard the funniest joke in the world.

"One day you're going to thank me for this," he said. "I'm only helping you."

I took a second to ask myself if it were real. Him, me, our marriage. Had I slept and woke up in another dimension? I was quiet for the entire ride back home and promised myself not to speak to him.

I drove past Ashland now, my chest growing tight in pain.

The memory of that day and many others would always be kept with me. I grabbed a hold of my phone to check the time. Marwa was expecting me. I'd be there in half an hour. I was so close to a fresh new start, away from him and every pain he ever afflicted me with. It had

9

been so long since I felt safe. Now I could finally taste that freedom again.

I struggled to remember a time when Khalid made me feel good about myself.

My best memories with him were before we got married, when he hadn't shown me his true colors. I told myself I should have known. It was like he was too good to be true. I couldn't help but feel so naive. The signs were all there, so why had I ignored them?

I tried taking my mind off of him and turned on the radio. I flipped through the FM channels but there was nothing worthwhile to listen to. I switched onto the CD player I had inside and played the first track on there. It was a mix of all my favorite Somali and English songs, a gift from my ex.

I knew what was coming but I needed to hear the words. I almost shut my eyes as the music poured out, attacking my broken soul. *Adele's* song was ripping me in places I never believed to have existed. I almost cried and then laughed at how silly this whole thing was. He would find me sooner or later; it was only a matter of time. Why was I even bothering to run away?

I tried to dissociate the things he made me believe about myself but that was difficult. He knew all the right things to say to break me. He was always ready to prove how powerless I was.

Once I had enough I turned off the radio and stopped at a red light. A young couple began walking through the crosswalk. They were hand in hand, each walking with a jump in their step. I wondered if he ever got jealous. Did he hold her hand because he wanted to let the world know she was his? Did he feel threatened when other men looked at her? Was he consumed with feelings of distrust and paranoia? I turned away from them once they reached the other side of the street.

I couldn't look at a couple without attributing the poison of my own relationship onto them. I had to accept that there were healthy and loving relationships out there. I had just been unfortunate to be stuck in a bad one. I hit the gas once the green light flashed. Only a couple more miles left until I reached Marwa's place. I knew I could count on her to provide me with a place to stay. She had her fair share of hurt in her own marriage, divorcing her husband three months ago. She told me they argued a lot, but I imagined it was nothing close to what Khalid made me endure. She was tough so I assumed she handled it pretty well. I didn't know how I would fair.

A part of me was grateful to start a new chapter in my life and another felt too crippled to do it alone. Khalid did more than bruise my face and body. He broke my confidence and self-esteem. I didn't value myself as much as I used to. I was a happier, more optimistic woman before I met him. Now I was shattered and torn to bits. This was my second failed relationship and the one that damaged me beyond repair.

I looked in the mirror at the fading bruise on my left cheek. The makeup wasn't doing a very good job of hiding it, especially not after all the tears. It hurt just as much as it did the first time. I would never forget the first time he hit me. It was as much a part of me as my name. As much as I tried to fight the pain of that day away I couldn't. I'd never forget.

Khalid had been away since Friday night, on a weekend trip with coworkers and bosses at a snow resort. It was Sunday night and he'd finally be coming back home to me.

I'd been preparing myself for his arrival all afternoon. I wanted to make sure every detail was just right and to his liking. So amongst other things that meant I cooked his all time favorite dish, fish steak and rice. I was going to serve it to him on the fine china too. For dessert he'd enjoy double chocolate fudge brownies I whipped up an hour earlier. I knocked out all the cleaning and laundry too. I had even gone out of my way to rent a couple of his favorite movies for later.

I also spent a good amount of time looking my best for Khalid. *Hooyo* had always reminded me that men were visual creatures who needed to be pleased with their eyes. In tune with that I straightened my hair, did my makeup, and wore a skin hugging dress I had lying around in my closet. It was a pretty crimson red that did a nice job of showing off my curves. Khalid wouldn't be able to take his eyes off me for the rest of the night.

There I was waiting on him to knock on the door and be in awe of the effort I went through for him. For once I wanted him to dote on me like good husbands were supposed to. I sat at the sofa with the DVDs on the coffee table next to a bowl of sweets. The house smelled of *Pine Sol* and burning candles and there I was at the center of it all.

After what seemed like a lifetime he finally came knocking at the door. I jumped up excitedly to go and greet him. Before I could get there he started buzzing the doorbell on repeat. I grew annoyed but told myself he may have needed to use the restroom. There could be no other explanation for him being so obnoxious.

I opened the door with a giant smile planted on my lips only to see an unfamiliar White man's face. It wasn't Khalid of course. I assumed he may have been the taxi driver.

"Good evening," the thin White man in a green polo shirt said. He seemed so sure of himself.

I looked past him to see Khalid glaring at me while making his way up the house steps. I was so confused. All of a sudden I noticed the strange man eyeing my body with no shame. That's when I remembered the tight dress I was wearing.

My face grew hot and embarrassment ate its way through me. Despite my unpleasant feelings I smiled and awkwardly made my way back into the house. I could already see Khalid putting me on blast later for his friend's staring. How was I to know he'd be bringing company?

After that I wanted to make myself invisible so I dashed away upstairs. I told myself I would only come back down once his company left. I listened for voices and then heard footsteps coming up the stairs. They were Khalid's. I knew the sound he made coming up all too well. I sat up expectantly in bed awaiting him.

He came to the door, stopped to glare at me and then vanished down the hall. I surged up and followed him. He was heading towards the guest bedroom, where he kept his work files. I watched while he went through his drawers looking for something unknown to me.

"Khalid, who's that guy downstairs and what are you looking for?" I asked expecting a quick answer.

"The boss man", he muttered under his breath.

"Okay. So why is he here?" It was a strange time for him to drop by.

He stopped looking for whatever he was trying to find and narrowed his eyes at me.

"Now is not the time for twenty one questions", he said with clenched teeth.

I frowned and leaned against the wall. I stood there clueless as Khalid dug through his files. After a short moment he stopped and sprinted out of the room with a stapled set of papers. He slammed the door after him, leaving me in utter confusion. I opened it after him and listened for a closing door. Once I heard it I went downstairs to investigate what just happened.

I found Khalid with his legs stretched apart on the sofa, with a dvd in hand. He looked a little less tense so I figured I could ask him. I sat at the other sofa and leaned forward, holding my hands together.

"So what was that all about?"

Khalid hunched forward as he set the DVD case onto the table.

"What's there to eat?" He asked yawning. I stared at him in complete disbelief.

"Khalid mind explaining to me?" I repeated impatient.

He grunted and sat back all of a sudden. I sat there foolishly expecting him to give me some kind of a response. When he wouldn't say anything I took it as my time to speak.

"I know you said he was your boss but what was he doing here? What did he need from you?"

Khalid reached into his pocket and pulled out his phone. He started scrolling and typing away like he hadn't just heard me ask him a question. He had some kind of nerve tonight.

"Wow. Are you being serious right now?" I was beyond annoyed. He never bothered to communicate with me but complained whenever I didn't tell him anything.

Khalid met my frustrated face with a nasty expression. It was the kind of look he made whenever he'd say something equally nasty and mean spirited. I expected his comments any minute. This time around I promised myself I wouldn't get emotional.

14

"Would you quit being such a pain in my ass? Why do you even care? Just bring me something to eat already," he said in a harsh tone. I watched in disgust as he slumped back in his seat to use his phone.

"Unbelievable. You're so full of it. You think because I'm not working now that I'm not worthy of telling things to?"

Khalid set his phone down and clasped his hands together. It was finally time for *him* to speak.

"That's exactly what I think. Now shut the hell up already and bring me some damn food!"

"Screw you Khalid. Get up and do it yourself. You think you're such a big shot don't you?"

I walked over to the armrest and dropped down into the chair. I had enough of his bad attitude. He thought he could talk to me any type of way he wanted. Well he was wrong if he thought he could get away with it this time around. I spent my whole day trying to impress him and this was the kind of thanks I got from his stupid ungrateful ass. I was done with trying to obey him and play nice wife.

Khalid laughed out loud. "I'm really not in the mood for this crap. First that and then this?"

I sat forward. "First what? What did I do wrong now? You just got back home and you're already scolding me like I'm your damn kid. Would you get a hold of yourself?"

He laughed some more. "You answer the door half-naked giving my boss a damn show is what. Don't you have any self respect? You just stood there and let him have a preview."

"Excuse me? How the hell was I supposed to know he'd turn up? You didn't exactly tell me!"

"I don't need to. Is that how you answer the door for the mailman too? You disgust me *wallahi*. *Sidaan isku dhaan* and bring me something to eat." I was shocked and speechless for a response.

"One, stop being so paranoid all the time. Two get up off your ass and do it yourself. You have hands, don't you?" I snapped back glaring at him, hoping to poison him with every bit of venom in my tone.

Khalid shot up to his feet and got in my face.

"*Nayaa* I don't find this funny! Now stop being such a nasty bitch and do your job!"

I simply smiled, possessing all the anger in the world. Two could play that game. I rose up and stuck out my middle finger as I stared at him dead in the eyes.

"How's that for bitch?" I asked, making my way towards the stairs. I didn't even get halfway there. Khalid grabbed me roughly and shoved me hard against the wall. My head rocked back and something in my neck vibrated.

"Who do you think you're talking to?" He whispered, breathing heavy.

I smiled, masking my fear. "Exactly. No one. You're pathetic."

In a quick motion he smacked me hard on my cheek leaving the right side of my face red as it burned in pain. The shock was more damaging than the initial feeling.

"What were you saying?" He asked with a taunting smile.

My eyes watered as I held the right side of my face in pain. I looked him in the eye and when he least expected it landed a mound of spit onto the tip of his nose. That should settle it I thought. I smiled satisfied as he shut his eyes in disgust. He was a germaphobe so I knew it was bound to enrage him.

Khalid grabbed me by my jaw and shook me violently.

"You disgusting bitch- apologize to me. Now!" Some of his spit landed inside of my eyes.

The words were unable to form on my lips so he shook me harder and smacked me again. My face was throbbing with hot pain. It was twice as hard as the last one. At that point something in me crumbled, and I no longer wanted to fight. The desire to was gone. Seconds later my chest began to heave up and down as I wept.

Khalid stepped back, watching me cover my face in complete humiliation. *How could he set his hands on me and treat me like I was so worthless? Why wasn't he mindful of the pain he inflicted on me? Did he no longer love me?* A million and one questions raced through my mind as I dropped down to my knees and sobbed to no end.

He said and did nothing until I began banging my hands against the floor. I must've really struck something in him then. In the next instant he rushed over and wrapped his arms around me.

"Baby...I'm sorry. I didn't mean to hurt you. I swear it'll never happen again. I'm so sorry."

Those same words would be uttered each and every time he laid his hands on me. It became as predictable as his lightning rage and frustration. They were words of convenience he used to try and lure me back into believing he was sincere. I never once allowed myself to believe him. I knew he was just as capable of lying to me as he was hurting me.

From then on the abuse became regular. Khalid was a man who was never happy with anything. It was like the whole world around him was this big fat inconvenience he was forced to put up with. Day after day he'd come home from work angry and berate me over the smallest things. I carried a ton of anxiety and fear in my chest whenever he was around. I always tried my best to slip away from him, especially after dinner time. That was when he was at his worst. It was like the food I made him only fueled his hatred towards me.

I blamed myself a lot. I found reasons to excuse his nasty words and beatings. It had to be my fault I'd say. Maybe I didn't greet him the way he wanted, or maybe the food was too salty. Maybe he was right for lashing out at me and treating me the way he did. The sorrow in my heart grew heavier each day I was with Khalid. I was helpless and in need of finding some kind of comfort in my life. I debated telling someone about the abuse. I knew Khalid would lose it if I did, but I could find ways of keeping it a secret. I cancelled out the idea of sharing it with close friends and family. I told myself it had to be an outsider, because they wouldn't see things from one side.

Unfortunately that plan of mine never panned out, and I was left to suffer alone. Some nights I would cry out to God and beg Him for His help. I would raise my hands up high, as the tears came pouring down my cheeks.

I begged Him to change Khalid and place love and mercy in his heart. I asked Him to protect me from Khalid's rage and beatings. I would pray for hours until I found some calm and then go to sleep.

One of the worst things had to be lying beside him in bed. It was beyond damaging to have the cause of my distress next to me peacefully asleep. Sometimes I couldn't handle the stress of it in my

18

mind and left to go sleep on the couch downstairs. I couldn't fall asleep next to him and fool myself into believing it was normal. The bed of a married couple was supposed to be a place of love and peace. I had neither of those things with Khalid so I wouldn't force myself to sleep next to him.

Remembering all the pain he made me endure broke my heart. To think he was the same man that had come to my home to ask for my parent's blessing in marrying me. To think I once loved him.

It was difficult to believe that I was getting away from him now. I would no longer have to tolerate him and his heartless behavior, so why was I still suffering inside?

I stopped for another red light and saw a billboard of a man holding a woman from behind while she laughed. In big red letters it read, "Happy and healthy couples are playful."

It was funny how often I was reminded of happy and healthy couples who loved each other more than the whole wide world. Why did I deserve to be hounded by all that when I was dealing with what I was? It wasn't fair, but now I knew I had the chance to finally get out. My time was now.

I looked back at the bulletin and wondered if Khalid's hard smacks and jabs counted as "playful." Or the few times I tried fighting back and protecting my dignity.

As I drove closer to Marwa's I was reminded of something my aunt once told me. It was a few years ago but never left my memory since. She said that Somalis once believed that when a man beats you it's out of pure love and jealousy. When he stops laying hands on you is the day you should question whether he still loves you or not.

There wasn't a single day that went by where I ever told myself his abuse equated to his love for me. I knew that his violence towards me could only come from a dark and bitter place of hatred. If he loved me it would show through his words and affection. I knew my Aunt was only relating some old wives tale to me, but it still hurt to think there were people who actually believed in that.

Here I was escaping him while some poor soul was probably clinging to her man and pushing him to beat her again. The world was a sad and twisted place in that way. I kept my eyes peeled on the road, as I drove through the next intersection. I pictured what Khalid would be doing at this very moment. What thoughts were going through his mind?

Today's events had been an eye opener for me. I finally understood why Khalid was the way he was. I re-imagined myself at the dining table with his parents, Ismail and Hanifa.

Khalid finished pouring some of the smoothie into a cup for his mother. I tried getting his attention then so he could get me some as well, but he wasn't even looking my way.

It was like I had gone completely invisible to him. I felt so silly for being there and playing my part in this perfect little couple act he was trying to pull. I saw his mother earlier, looking at the fading bruise on my cheek. His parents weren't deaf and blind to what was going on between him and me. So why did he insist on thinking they would be? I told myself to just stick this thing out for his mother's sake. She had gone out of her way to invite us over for lunch and prepare us such a big meal. As I sat there picking at my rice, I tried picking up on what was not being said.

Khalid had been bragging about his job and income to his parents for so long now. His dad was obviously proud as was his mother. The only thing was Khalid didn't seem to be as happy about that as I would expect for him to be. His parents clearly adored him and yet he seemed so indifferent.

His father, Ismail was a very respected and reserved man. And yet he was going out of his way to make me feel comfortable. Khalid's mother, Hanifa was also very sweet and considerate. I couldn't help but wonder how Khalid wound up being such a horrible person with parents like his. I peered up and smiled at his mother who was looking at me from across the table.

I put a spoonful of rice into my mouth. I wanted some smoothie to drink, but didn't want to ask. So I insisted on staring at the vessel until someone eventually noticed. Surprisingly, it was his father, Ismail who did.

"*Allah*! Get the girl something to drink Khalid. Be mindful of your wife!" He proclaimed.

Khalid looked up at me from his plate and quickly poured me a helping.

My hand trembled as I reached out to grab the glass from him. There were some things I couldn't even hide around his parents. For a moment it felt like his mother was looking at me again, but she had only been staring off into the distance.

I drank and continued eating my food in silence. I wondered what his mother was thinking about. I looked back at her and then to Khalid. He was eating like he'd never had a home cooked meal in years. I could see his parents exchanging looks at one another. I was mortified.

"*Hooyo*, would you like some more?" Hanifa asked, grabbing an edge of the bowl of rice.

Khalid nodded and handed her his plate. I watched closely as she gave him a generous second helping.

I felt so annoyed with him. I cooked for him each and every day, and yet he wanted to make it seem like I was starving him back home. Him giving me the cold shoulder was enough, but this was just pushing it. Khalid's dad chuckled and shook his head amused.

"*Hee, Aabo?* What is it?" Khalid asked grinning from ear to ear.

"Nothing. I just like your enthusiasm is all. You must be really hungry," Ismail commented grinning.

Khalid smiled and looked to me. I knew what was coming. I turned to look at his mother who was making a face at him, almost disapproving whatever stupid thing was going to come out of his mouth.

"Well, it's not every day I get to eat like this *Aabo*. I'm just being appreciative." He was smirking.

I had it. It was as if his mother knew just what I was thinking and made eyes at me to stay seated. I silently obeyed and remained put in my chair. I dropped my fork down onto my plate, losing my appetite.

Ismail smiled. "What is this Amilah? You don't ever cook for my son?"

"*Aabo*, if you only knew," Khalid muttered under his breath. "I feel like a *prisoner*."

Hanifa stepped in at that point. "Khalid, that's enough now. Don't speak ill of your wife."

Khalid shrugged and smiled smugly. "What can I say? I'm just being honest."

My heartbeat was racing and I felt like lunging at him and calling him all the nastiest names I could think of. How could he disrespect me in front of his parents? It was bad enough I came here, and now he wanted to make me suffer. I clenched my fists tightly as I glared at him.

"Let the boy speak his mind," Ismail said scowling at his wife.

She sighed. "I won't. Not if it's coming at the expense of his own wife. He crossed a line just now and you know it."

Ismail groaned, and sipped away at his drink. I was starting to see a lot of Khalid in him. Apart from the identical jaw line and almond shaped eyes, they shared a similar bad attitude. It was beginning to make so much sense to me now. Like father, like son.

I could picture a younger Khalid looking at his father at this same table, emulating and revering his every action. I felt sick to my stomach. There was something in the air that started to feel so suffocating.

His mother kept her gaze down. Khalid looked remorseful, like he knew now that he shouldn't of spoken so carelessly. I despised him in that moment more than any other, but a small part of me wondered at him. There was a look in his eyes that showed some vulnerability.

"This isn't the U.N. You don't need to speak for anyone," Ismail grumbled, in an angry tone.

We all turned to look at him then. I could see this escalating already. Khalid had really done it this time. He didn't know when to keep his privileged little mouth shut. Now he would have to face the consequences of what he instigated.

"I can speak up for whoever I like. This is my home as much as it's yours," Hanifa said. I was surprised by her, as was Khalid. It wasn't very often you heard her speak back to him. In the few times I was around them she had always been so silent and obedient to everything he said.

Ismail looked enraged. I could see the fire building in his eyes. He was looking at his wife with such hate, it haunted me to my core. I hoped that only words would be exchanged and nothing more.

"*Aabo*...please," Khalid began in a shaky voice. *Now* he wanted to speak up?

"Shut up," Ismail snapped back. "You don't get in between your mother and me. Don't you ever learn?"

I coughed, almost trying to let them know that they still had me around. It was getting so uncomfortable that I decided to get up and just leave. I couldn't be around this anymore, it felt too strange.

"Where are you going?" Hanifa asked sharply. Khalid and his father both turned at once. Now all the attention was on me. This was proving to be a little too much for me now.

I hesitated. "Umm...I was just about to...umm...uhh."

"Stay put," She remarked, with firmness in her voice. She looked dead serious, like she had this whole thing under control. I obeyed and sat back down. Once I did she twisted her head back towards her husband.

"Now listen to me. You don't tell me how to speak to my own son. I'm his mother."

Khalid coughed and cleared his throat. "C'mon now...let's keep it calm."

His words went unnoticed by his parents, and I really couldn't help but picture him as that poor ignored child in the middle of his bickering parents' disputes. Now he was reliving those days again and had me around as another witness.

"Don't you disrespect me like this," Ismail said sternly. He balled up his hands as a single vein emerged from his temple.

I grabbed my glass and took a sip, as the air around me grew fainter. This was not going anywhere. Why couldn't they just stop all this before it got any worse? Khalid had no impact on them and neither would I. I looked at him suddenly, as he met my gaze. He instantly looked away and fumbled with the fork on his plate.

"There's no disrespect on my side. I was just speaking to my son," Hanifa said.

Ismail laughed. "This has gone far enough. Let's just keep it civil for their sake."

She laughed too. "You wouldn't know anything about that. Let's not pretend now."

With that said she rose, nodded her head to me respectfully and walked out of the room. I looked towards his father who was clenching his jaw and looking as if he had a bad taste of something in his mouth. Khalid reached his hand out toward his father's but he only shook it away.

Within seconds Ismail got up as well, marching after his wife down the hall. I looked at Khalid for some kind of an explanation, but he looked just as lost as me. I felt bad for him but told myself this was nothing close to what he made me endure. The room went silent with neither of us speaking and then came the shouting. Khalid and I both looked to each other with fear creeping into our eyes.

There was a door slam and a loud crashing noise. It sounded like something had been thrown across the room. My eyes started to grow wet all of a sudden.

"You stupid woman! Won't you ever learn?!" I heard Ismail shout. His words were followed by a loud bang. My heart skipped a beat as I recognized it to be a hard slap. His poor wife.

Khalid shot up and then sat back down. I watched as he shook and covered his hands over his face.

"Khalid-I think you should…," I began with a shaking voice.

"Shut up! I don't want to hear a single word out of you. Don't speak to me now."

I opened and closed my mouth, struggling for the right words to say. Why was he lashing out on me now? None of this was my fault. If anything he was in the wrong for instigating a problem in the first place. Now his mother was suffering at the hands of his father.

"Khalid…I don't understand," I began saying. "I'm sorry but I didn't do anything wrong."

"Stop! Stop talking alright?! I'm tired of hearing your disgusting voice." He was glaring hard at me.

Something hit me then. I didn't need to apologize and try and make sense of him, or our marriage anymore. If this wasn't a clear sign for me then I didn't know what would be. I wasn't going to get on my knees and apologize for something I had nothing to do with.

Everything started coming together. The pigmented pieces inside my mind finally formed into a complete picture. I was going to leave

Khalid. I wasn't going to sit and wait by his side until he got some sense knocked back into him. I wasn't going to be like his mother. I sighed and got up, heading straight for the front door.

I waited to hear him call me back and tell me he was sorry. But there was none of that, just more daunting silence. I didn't waste a single moment and stole his keys from his jacket pocket. I left the house, got into the car and drove back home. I'd collect all my things and make my exit from this so called marriage. I had plans for myself and Khalid was no longer a part of them.

With Marwa's home now in sight, I smiled gratefully. This was my first small victory in so long. I wanted to celebrate this moment, the end to this marriage. I wanted to live freely and without fear again. My mother always told me that life was short and better spent living happily.

I grabbed my bag and made my way towards Marwa's front door. There was a heavy feeling that was lifted off of my chest. It had been a long time coming but now I could breathe again. I knocked and waited for her to open the door, impatient and expectant. I'd embrace her like the good friend she was and be welcomed into a home of peace, kindness, and safety. A home free of any pain, abuse or heartache. Free of Khalid and all the worries he ever plagued me with.

I knocked on the door and waited eagerly. The sun was shining its rays down upon me, and I hadn't felt short of blessed. I was lucky to be standing where I was, far and away from Khalid's venom.

There were footsteps at the other side of the door. My heart was leaping with joy as I imagined the kind smile of my beautiful friend Marwa. We'd heal together. Divorce wasn't going to be the end of us. The aches and pains could be sewn over, and I planned to do that a day at a time. *Together.* For now the next chapter of my life was calling, and I was ready to give it my full attention.

Monkeying Around

After 9/11, no one wanted anything to do with the Muslim kids at school. Everyone avoided them like the plague. I'll admit they had it pretty rough. No one knew much about Islam, but recognizing a Muslim was as easy as spotting the school stoner. They had their culture wound around them- names and clothes and all. It made it all the easier for people to rip into them with insults.

I never really meant to befriend Mohamed.

The crew I rolled with had always been the same group of guys I took my first swimming lessons with. Sailing through high school I had imagined that would never change. Mohamed and I shared first period Chemistry together - when I made it to class, that is. I had this habit of coming late after my dad was released from the hospital. Recovering from pneumonia meant dad depended upon all the help my mother, brother, and I could give him.

Each morning I helped dad out of bed, adjusted his breathing machine, and prepared him breakfast. It cut a good thirty minutes into my first period. Luckily my brother would come home from his PM shift in time for me to borrow his car and catch the last part of chem. Anyway, Mohamed was a pretty quiet kid. I could tell he was smart because he always got his tests papers handed back first. Unlike a lot of us he didn't spend class time dozing off.

Mr. Barnes would lecture to the class but you could tell he was only looking in his general direction. I understood it as him giving priority to the kid who actually cared to learn. Mohamed was the brainiac type to know all the answers and still wait a few seconds before saying anything. I always thought that pretty decent of a kid who was surrounded by so many slackers, myself included.

28

Time and time again I ended up having to pair with Mohamed. He was always off on his own. Things had been pretty tense after the attacks and no one wanted to be caught cozying up with the "enemy". I didn't have much of a problem with him. He minded his own business and helped me whenever I needed it. Not to mention he'd do a crapload of the in-class assignments for me. Most mornings I sat back and let Mohamed do all the work while scarfing down a pack of blueberry *Pop Tarts*.

At one point in the school year I remember Mohamed asking me if I had ever watched wrestling. It was the one time he spoke to me about non-Chem. related stuff and it had to be about wrestling. In all honesty I hated it. I never could make sense of why people would willingly watch a fake match between two overly greased morons. Being stuck with that crap while I waited for the good stuff to come on TV was the bane of my existence.

Mohamed gave me a fist bump and turned his attention to Mr. Barnes who was shooting darts at me from the front of the class. I wasn't winning any points with him for sure. Only I liked to think Mohamed was warming up to me. For one, I didn't make a big deal of having to partner up with him. Plus I showed some interest in the subject and thanked him for his help. I was a saint compared to the guys who called him *"Osama's son"* from the back of class. I think he may have even considered me a good friend. Unlike the other kids I talked to him and even put my neck on the line for him once.

Of course Mohamed hadn't known and I wasn't going to bother ever telling him either.

It happened the other week during English class. Halfway through the period I had to really go pee. So I excused myself from class and sped towards the nearest restroom. With my classroom being smack dab in the center of school that left me with two options. The first was a bathroom around the corner nearest to the vending machines. It was one of the filthiest places on campus. Men's bathrooms were hardly ever clean but this God forsaken one took the cake. Luckily there was another bathroom, and it was near the front of campus. That was the one actually safe for human use. Sprinting at full speed I contemplated going into the filth pit, curious to what type of deadly disease I could pick up in there.

With just a few inches away from my destination I noticed someone under the shade of the tree in front of the school. From where I was standing I had a good view of the flagpole, parking lot and whatever the heck this person was doing only a few feet away from me.

Minutes away from soiling myself I stopped to take in the scene. Some kid with a green mat laid onto the ground doing some strange bendy movements. It took me a second longer to realize it'd been none other than Mohamed. His hair was shorter than I remembered it earlier in the week. I watched in confusion as he proceeded to dropping his forehead onto the ground, placing his hands flat onto the mat. It was one of the weirdest things I'd ever seen in my life.

He got up all of a sudden and then dropped his head back down. He kept his head on the ground for what seemed like an eternity. I realized he may have been doing some kind of prayer or ritual type thing. I remembered seeing something similar on the *National Geographic* channel once. Dad was trying his best to explain it to me. He liked to think of himself as culturally aware after a stint in the navy.

"What the hell?!" Some kid cried out piercing my ears with his screeching voice.

I turned around to see a party of three guys behind me. I hadn't been sure how long they'd been standing there and watching. It could have been around the same time as me or maybe even longer. A bad feeling began to creep inside my stomach and I felt like I was going to be sick.

Another one of the guys let out a nasty harsh laugh. There was some mumbling but I wasn't entirely sure what was being said by them. In the next instant I saw a big wad of spit flying onto the ground. Their footsteps were drawing closer. The possibility of them doing something awful to Mohamed hit me and I knew I needed to act fast. He had still been sitting when I looked back at him last and now he was getting up again. I wished he'd have wrapped up his thing minutes ago. Hadn't he realized the threat only a few yards behind him?

"You guys just watch and learn. I'll show you how it's done." I heard one of the guys say.

"Poor little *Aladdin* and his stupid magic carpet." Another of them said followed by loud maniacal laughter. All of a sudden I turned around to the three guys and managed to move my lips a part despite the insane pounding of my chest.

"He's completely crazy," I said as the trio stopped in their tracks to look at me.

"What?" The tallest of the bunch said.

I sighed. "He's supposed to be on suspension but he won't get off campus. They're gonna call security on him soon. I wouldn't try anything. They'll be here any minute now."

One of the guys with a dictator mustache stepped up.

"What'd he get suspended for?"

"Probably trying to bomb his class!" The short chubby one said laughing hard.

"He's psycho but it wasn't anything like that. I heard it was a fight. Some guys tried jumping him after school one day and he surprised

31

them with his brass knuckles. Two of em' got sent to the ICU in the same ambulance."

All three of the guys fell silent as they looked fearfully ahead at Mohamed. He was all finished now and neatly folding up his mat, stuffing it into his backpack. These guys were a con artist's dream come true. Complete gullible idiots. Anyone else could see Mohamed had the nature of a shy squirrel with people phobia. He was the last type of person to threaten or harm somebody.

"What a nutcase," the short one muttered.

"C'mon let's get going before security shows up," the tall one said, leading the pack back in the direction they had come from.

I turned back to Mohamed who was pulling on the straps of his backpack now. Didn't he know any better than to do that kind of thing out in the open? Especially so soon after the terrorist attacks. I breathed a sigh of relief. The urge to pee set back in and I made my way to the restroom.

I thought of what may have happened to Mohamed had I not been there. The three stooges could have easily beaten the crap out of him and gotten away with it. School security was a joke and they made it their priority to be as uninvolved as possible.

Whatever the case, I was glad to have seen him walk away in one piece.

****

By the time October rolled around, everyone was talking Halloween. For a bunch of high schoolers that translated into partying and guzzling lethal amounts of alcohol. The days of trick-or-treating were long gone with our sweet tooth's finally fading away. My friends and I had our sights set on crashing all the varsity squad parties. Everyone knew that if you wanted booze - the varsity parties were the way to go. There would of course be a ton of hot girls and no one could argue against that.

So when talk of the biggest beef head of the school hosting a party got out, we were game. Everyone was going to be there and my friends and I were no exception. In the weeks leading up to the bash, people wouldn't stop talking about how badass it was going to be. My friends and I would finally be able to revel in what the other side got to have on a regular basis.

Talk had it that people would only be let in based on the quality of their costumes. It was all or nothing for us. People were already saying beef head didn't want a lot of guys there, so we knew our costumes had to be mind blowing. Our entrance was completely dependent on it.

At first we considered going in as *Marvel* characters but shot that idea down fast. A bunch of zeros draped in hero costumes wasn't going to win the admiration of anyone. We'd just seem pathetic. Then like a light bulb it went off in our dim little heads. We'd come in as a bunch of terrorists! The time was a bit too soon with 9/11 just a month earlier but we still told ourselves we could pull it off. The thing was, we wanted our costumes to look authentic. None of us wanted to settle for some crap from the dollar store. It was going to be tricky and so we took it very seriously.

We kept telling ourselves people wouldn't be able to stop talking about us for months to come. No doubt we'd get some well deserved attention from the ladies as well. The only problem was we had no idea where to get the kinds of Middle Eastern clothes we were looking for. So being the nerds my friends were at the time, they wanted to settle for coming in as *Marvel* characters after all. I would have ended up doing the same had I not seen Mohamed's dad show up to school.

It had been a long day of hearing teachers yap and I was glad to finally be free. Anticipating the reunion with my bed, I dragged my feet to the parking lot. While making my way there I noticed a tall, dark man who looked to be around my dad's age. Only he was dressed nothing like he ever would. He was wearing a long white robe with a matching white hat over his head. I kept asking myself where I'd seen that kind of thing before. Like a ton of bricks it hit me. On the news!

The terrorists overseas wore those same kinds of clothes. My dad said it was their cultural norm. I couldn't get my head around it, but I guess it beat wearing denim all day. In that moment I asked myself why the hell the man had been standing there in the first place. I realized it was after school, and he could have been waiting on someone. It wasn't long before I noticed Mohamed racing in the direction of the man. *He was his son.* Not even a minute later some guys caught wind of Mohamed's dad standing there and went into full attack mode.

"Sand-nigger! Camel jockey! Towel head! Osama bin Laden!"

The insults were raining in and I felt genuinely bad for Mohamed's dad. The kids all being assholes weren't going to let Mohamed live this down. I knew it would be recycled for tomorrow and the next day to come. They were jerks like that.

Coming home that day from school I gave it a lot of thought. I could still dress up as a terrorist like originally planned. I'd look like a real one too, all thanks to Mohamed. I figured he could lend me one of those long robe things and something to wear over my head.

I'd get some fake guns and dynamite from the party shop. Then the rest would be history. People would envy my costume for years to come. I'd be a school legend! Luckily Mohamed seemed to like me enough for me to get away with it. I'd just lie and tell him it was for another friend. I knew he would give in, so I asked him one day after Chem. class. He gave me the strangest look.

He shut his binder slowly and grinned. "What do you want it for?"

34

"I think it's kind of cool and aren't they pretty comfortable? I've got to tell you, wearing jeans all day isn't really doing it for me." I shot him the most charming smile I could muster.

Mohamed saw right through the lies I was feeding him. He was a pretty smart guy after all.

He asked plainly. "You want to dress up as a terrorist for the party, don't you?"

I immediately began to apologize until Mohamed interrupted me.

He said he didn't really care and asked when I'd come over to his to pick it up. Just like that, and it was a deal. I was really starting to like Mohamed and this developing friendship of ours. I secretly wondered if he thought it would be a badass costume himself.

One day after class I walked with Mohamed to his place. The kids at school saw this and started popping off with the terrorist jokes. It was like Groundhog Day all over again.

Some kid wearing a giant black hoodie shouted, "Hey stay away from Osama!"

"Don't let the towel head bomb you!" A kid in basketball shorts chimed in.

Another boy standing nearby cried out, "Dirty sand nigger-loving fruitcake!"

Mohamed and I shrugged them off and kept on to the path to his. Surprisingly he didn't happen to live too far from school. I even recognized the route there from a time when I used to run the paper route in the same neighborhood.

"My dad is usually out right about now. He got laid off from his job and won't tell my mom. So, he pretends to be out working during the day...I don't know why I'm telling you this."

"No, it's cool man. Is it because…?" I tried to be gentle about asking.

Mohamed shook his head. "Six other people got laid off in the same week. It's just a crappy job."

I laughed. "Oh. *Gotcha.*"

We kept on the way to his until we stopped at a one story auburn-colored place. It was nice and quaint. Looked like something my mom would've wanted for us.

"You have to take your shoes off. They're just rules." Mohamed said seriously.

I stopped and did as he asked. Coming in, I was greeted with the smell of delicious smelling food cooking. I got so distracted by the aroma that I tripped on a mountain-high stack of shoes. Luckily, I caught my balance before I could fall face first on the sprawling red carpet.

These rules are going to land someone with a busted ass if they aren't careful, I thought.

Mohamed exchanged a look with me. "I think there might be guests over. Hold on. I'll go check." I did as I was told and stayed close to the door.

Mohamed walked out into the living room, leaving me alone with the pile of shoes.

There were family pictures on the wall, a sugar jar, and a box of *Twinkies* on the counter. If only the kids at school had seen just how regular this place looked. Then maybe they wouldn't believe half the crap they thought about Mohamed and his family.

"C'mon let's go upstairs," he said, returning from the living room.

I followed him there, but first took a peek into the living area. There were a group of men and women drinking from tea cups and speaking in a language I had never heard. I remember Mohamed saying he was from some place in Africa, but hadn't remembered exactly where.

"They all your family?" I asked Mohamed, who was steps ahead of me.

"Distant but still related I guess." He led us down the hallway to a closed door.

"I have it in my room. Snuck it out of my dad's closet last night," he said over his shoulder as he opened the door to his room.

"Oh nice." I replied, suddenly feeling guilty. It was as if half of the weight of the assholery I was committing hit me all at once.

Mohamed opened the door to his room, and I took a second to look around. There were posters of *Star Wars* and a *NASA* sticker posted over his bed frame. At another part of the room was a whole shelf of books and clothes scattered all over the floor. For a second, it didn't look so much different than my own room.

I watched as he grabbed a bag of clothes from his closet and then held it out to me.

"Thanks." I muttered, glancing at his face to see his expression. He didn't look like he was offended.

"Yeah man. No problem." I took the bag from his hands.

Afterward Mohamed fell onto his bed, and reached for his *Game boy*.

"Is that all or can I tempt you to lose in some video games?"

I laughed. "Nah man. I better get going. My mom's gonna be pissed if I'm not back soon."

Mohamed shrugged and turned his eyes back to his handheld. I took one more look around his room.

"Cool room."

"Thanks." He replied, barely looking up.

"See you tomorrow, man," I said before turning towards the door.

Mohamed cleared his throat and sat up. "Try not to get noticed by my mom. She'll try keeping you over for dinner."

I grinned. "Yeah man. Maybe next time."

"Seeya," I said before finally leaving his room. I looked down at the bag in my hands. For a split moment, my conscience demanded my attention. Was dressing up as a terrorist really the best costume I could think up? Especially after the attacks that had happened a month before.

I thought back to the other day at school when Mohamed's dad showed up and how the kids at school viciously went at him. I thought of Mohamed. He was a cool guy and all. Then I thought of myself, at the center of everything. I was probably the first person after the attacks to talk to Mohamed at school. And the first person to ask to wear his parents clothes as a costume. I realized how messed up it all was.

But I had the clothes in my hand and it was too late to go as someone else now.

****

It was Judgment Day. The night of the Halloween bash had finally arrived. I mentally and physically prepared myself for the mayhem that would later ensue. I couldn't stop thinking about the love my costume would receive. At lunch, I pushed myself to avoid any of the greasy crap they were serving. I knew it wouldn't bode well with me after a night of drinking. My friends did the opposite, and went for seconds of the pizza and fries.

After school, I drove home feeling like I was on cloud nine. I kept thinking about the looks people would have on their faces when they'd see me - awe, respect, and maybe some appreciation from the ladies. Some girls probably wouldn't want to be anywhere near me.

Understandable. I suppose the fun ones would come my way and that's all that mattered.

I thought about Mohamed, too. He had been quiet in first period and hardly said anything to me. A part of me wondered if there were any hard feelings. He didn't seem to mind me asking for the clothes at his house. He didn't hesitate to lend them to me, either, so we had to be cool. Right? When I got home I checked on my dad in his room. Like usual, he was staring blankly out his window.

"Hey." My voice brought him back to the present moment.

Dad turned slowly over towards me and smiled. "Hey son, how was your day?"

I stepped into the room and began messing with an old rubix cube on the table.

"It was alright. Yours?" The sound from his breathing machine filled in the awkward gaps in our conversation.

"Minus the bad lungs it wasn't too bad. Plus, your brother made lasagna for dinner."

"Made?" I grimaced. For as long as I had lived with him, my brother had never cooked a damn thing in his whole life.

Dad grinned. "Yes, made. You should try some. It's not so bad."

"Whatever you say, dad. Need anything? I'm heading to a Halloween thing later. I gotta get ready." I tried to fit all of it into one breath, so maybe he wouldn't catch everything I said.

He sat up with some difficulty. "'Thing'? Tell me about that."

Before I could he began coughing, really hard and for a good minute, too. I quickly poured him a glass of water and handed him his breathing tube. It helped his lungs do a better job of being lungs.

"Thanks," he managed, accepting the cold glass from my hand.

I waited for him to take a sip. "So, is it some kind of party?"

"Yeah. Just between some of my friends and me. Nothing wild." I wondered if he could tell that I was lying through my teeth.

He nodded. "I take it the whole school's going to be there. Can you promise me you won't drink and drive? That's my only condition for you to go."

"Dad, I'm not some idiot," I protested, pretending to be offended.

He didn't blink. I cleared my throat and crossed my arms in surrender. "I won't drink and drive. Happy?"

"Ask your brother to drop you off and pick you up," he said sternly.

"Do I look like I'm twelve? Dad, you can't be serious."

"I'm totally serious. Unless you'd like to walk home and back. Is it that far?" He reached for his glass.

"It's a few blocks north. I guess I could." I muttered going along with his bright idea.

"Keys?" Dad asked holding out his hand to me. He was dead serious about this.

I sighed, shaking my head. Incredible. Fishing through my pocket I retrieved them and dropped them into his hands.

"There you go." I said mimicking a happy voice. I wanted to snatch them back and walk out but knew better than to. After all he was sick and only worried about me coming home safe.

Dad grinned. "Atta boy. You have a fun time now. Don't do anything I wouldn't do."

"Yeah dad because that's the motto of my life." I replied much to his amusement.

I left the room to him chuckling and then coughing down to a quick silence.

****

Fresh out of the shower I decided not to shave and leave the five o'clock shadow that was beginning to creep over my face. It could be an authentic look. No one would think I was a real terrorist without any facial hair anyway. After applying some deodorant I reached for the long robe thing, and slipped it quickly on. No fuss at all. I was a happy camper.

Next I put on the baggy grey pants and topped the look with a white skull cap. Mohamed mentioned it was called a "*kufi*" but it passed for one all the same. I looked into the bag for anything more but there was nothing. So I went into my room and grabbed the fake dynamite and began wrapping it around my body. For some reason it felt like something was missing. I couldn't quite figure out what and grabbed the fake AK from my bedpost. I took a long look at myself and decided I looked completely ridiculous. The fake terrorist look was anything but cool. The dynamite and AK may have been a bit too much.

I quickly stripped away the fake dynamite and left the toy gun where it was. This worked much better and didn't look like I was trying so hard. I looked just like Mohamed's dad did that day at school. He was a real Muslim so I guess that was a good thing. I could imagine my dad would have a heart attack if he saw me. So I made sure his bedroom door was closed when I passed by. Mom was taking a shower so that gave me enough time to sneak out of the house problem free.

While outside I looked at myself in the reflection of my brother's car.

Moustafa. No, Ahmed.

I decided I'd have a fake name for the night and add to the costume more. I looked on at the car wishing I could be driving it but remembered the promise I made earlier with dad. So I walked on ahead and made my way to the party that would either make or break my final

42

year of high school. The streets were mostly empty, and that was strange for a Halloween night. There weren't too many people who had their lights on anyway. So I assumed it wasn't the first destination for any trick or treaters. I went along my way and felt sort've funny as I walked. If the kids at school could see me now they'd trash me for sure. Walking into an airport dressed the way I was would undoubtedly land me in custody too.

Along with the robe and hat I wore some slippers. There was definitely an *Aladdin* vibe about them, but I didn't mind them very much. It was nice and comfy wearing them, and I liked that.

I hadn't spoken to my friends recently and assumed they were on route like me. None of them knew who I would go dressed as. So they were going to be in for the surprise of their lives.

I walked confident as I made my way down the dimly lit residential neighborhoods. The area seemed so unfamiliar to me even though it was just a few blocks from my own house. I went over the moment I would walk into the party and the time in which I'd leave. Hopefully the differences were going to be major and not some disappointing fail.

Guys like me weren't incredibly good looking, smart, popular, or talented. All I had was to live off a moment. A single incredibly mind blowing moment which could surge me into another point in life I'd never experienced before. My friends were okay with just having a couple of beers and eyeing the cheerleaders. They'd talk about how wasted they got and how some hot chick was totally checking them out. I'd have to hear about if for weeks, and they could very well go on for months.

I wanted something different. *All eyes on me.* That kind of thing was something I sort've lived by in my younger days. In elementary I prepared myself for the popularity I told myself I'd reach in middle school. All through middle school I kept looking forward to being

43

thrust into the high school limelight. Neither seemed to ever happen for me. Looking back I always craved the attention, the reactions, and *eyes*. Maybe this moment would be it for me.

I continued down the sidewalk until I reached an area that didn't seem too familiar. I wondered if I took a wrong turn somewhere. I decided to walk back from where I started and try figuring out from there. I wouldn't have gotten lost in the first place if dad hadn't banned me from driving to the damn party.

Now I was going to turn up late, and miss out on all the fun.

I'd probably get there when everyone was drunk and puking all over the place. No one was going to care about anyone's costume then. I was screwed.

"Hey Abu! Ay you stupid Arab bastard!" A man shouted out.

Confused and alarmed I turned around to see two men at the end of the street. I thought of ignoring them and flipped them the bird. What a bunch of low lives they must have been. Hadn't they realized it was Halloween night? It wasn't everyday someone dressed like me decided to go out for a stroll at night. I wasn't going to give them any more thought or attention. They were probably just a pair of drunk bros unwinding from a night's partying. I continued on down the path I was going until I heard a strange noise behind me.

The hairs on my neck began to rise as I quickly turned back around in their direction.

They were running towards me at full speed. My heart began to beat uncontrollably, to the point where it felt like I was going to pass out. A sense of panic and fear struck down on me as I fumbled to get my body to move. The two of them were both hefty and close to my dad's size. It almost looked like one was carrying an object in his hand.

My legs finally seemed to turn on again and I started bolting away from them.

"Come here Osama! We just wanna talk!" One of the men hollered.

Judging from his voice they weren't very far behind. I tried to keep my calm as my legs grew tired of running. I tried to think positive as I sought out a place of safety I was stranger to. I didn't know this neighborhood and it was dark out. Where was I going to go?

Buckets of sweat falling off my face, arms, and legs, I asked myself if this were really happening to me. My face grew red hot as the cold night's air whipped against me. Fortunately for me I was faster and younger than they were but much more afraid.

As I turned into another neighborhood I frantically turned back around to hardly see the men behind me. I took the moment to finally slow down and catch my breath. With heavy breaths I wrestled to take the clothes off and left only a tank top and the baggy pants on. I tossed the hat into some bushes and began down the path towards home. The streets had finally started to look familiar to me again, and I felt safe.

I could easily make out my house now, and a feeling of peace began to wash over me.

For a moment I could still hear the men coming after me. A part of me told myself they were waiting around somewhere and would pounce when I looked the most unnoticing. When I reached my doorway I took one last final look around. I lost them a long ways back and prayed they were no longer anywhere near me. It had been my own life for a freaking *Halloween* costume.

Taking a deep breath I dug out my set of house keys from the baggy pants pocket and wrestled with the doorknob to get inside. The lights inside the house were nearly dim, and I knew dad and mom must have been asleep. I locked the door and very paranoidly checked a few times to make sure. Once I was assured it was in fact locked I quietly made my way up the stairs to my bedroom. I needed a nice long shower after what I'd been through tonight.

My legs had been so exhausted from all the running I had to do. I never knew I could run so fast in my life. Maybe this was my introduction to track and field. Maybe those morons had done me a favor by helping me figure out what I was actually good at.

I felt grateful to have finally reached the comfort of my warm home and more so completely unharmed. As I laid out on my bed, my mind raced back to Mohamed and his family. His dad seemed so indifferent to all the nasty names the kids at school were calling him. It was like he'd just grown used to it. I wasn't a Muslim and would never understand the kind of stuff they went through, but if it were anything like tonight it must have been hell. I remembered back to the day at school too.

Mohamed would have gotten jumped had I not been there. For a second I wondered if I had bumped into the fathers of those idiots tonight. Maybe the brothers or even uncles. One thing was for sure wearing Mohamed's dad's clothes for a single night was nothing like walking in his shoes. I knew they were growing through it after the attacks but never imagined how bad it could be.

Dad said we weren't even seeing the worst of it. He told me the whole country was gonna be riled up, and that we could maybe even go to war. I didn't want to think so dark about it but guessed there could be a good chance of that. All I knew was I screwed up tonight, and for the future I was done *monkeying around*.

HANIYA

Fresh outta high school I had believed it to be a case of the "senioritis." I started out getting upset by the smallest things and withdrawing from family and friends. By the time I was nineteen I was having fits of tears nearly every day. I would lock myself in my room and weep into my pillow until I fell asleep. At twenty I contemplated suicide and attempted it a few weeks after I turned twenty one.

I stupidly left the bathroom door unlocked and my younger sister walked in. The sound of her high-pitched shriek sent shockwaves throughout my body. The kitchen knife I held in my hand fell as she went racing down the hall. It wasn't long before it was brought to the attention of my other siblings and parents. That same day my mother and father barged into my room and interrogated me for two whole hours.

"What's so wrong with your life that you would try to kill yourself?" *Hooyo* managed to ask me while half crying and yelling.

"What haven't we given you in life? What did we do to make you so unhappy?" She barked at me moments later.

"*Raali ahow,*" was all I could mutter in response.

"Are we bad parents?" My father asked, his voice shaking.

"No, *raali ahow.*" I mumbled again and again. "Forgive me."

My parents were relentless as they reminded me of what they had to endure back in Somalia. *Hooyo* went on and on about the many miserable days of hunger, fear, travelling at night and being helpless. The effect she was seeking in me worked as I grew incredibly guilty. In their raging voices they demanded to know how someone as privileged as me could ever feel depressed. Afterwards, they began throwing out

47

random accusations and assumed I was in some kind of serious trouble.

"Are you part of a gang?" *Aabo* spat with frustration.

"No." I quickly answered, not blinking.

"Are you failing in school? Did you get probation like your brother?" He further questioned.

"Do you have a boyfriend? Did you become pregnant?" My mother joined in.

Mortified I finally spoke up. "What? Are you serious?!" My mother was ready to counterattack when *Aabo* grabbed hold of her shoulder.

He mumbled something to my mother I couldn't hear as I breathed a sigh of relief. I thought maybe he could still recognize the look of innocence in me. The "meeting" was wrapped up by me promising to never repeat what I failed to complete. They warned me if I ever did then I would spend an eternity being punished in *jahannam*. Not only that but I would bring endless shame to the family in this lifetime. With a perplexed look, my mother asked me if that was the kind of thing I wanted to make them endure.

"Do you want to shame the family name? Do you want people to talk endlessly about us?" She asked me unable to hold back her falling tears. Tears of guilt fell out of my own eyes as I shook my head and muttered a weak "no."

The following weekend *Quran* was read upon me. In a loose black *abaya* and matching *jilbaab* I sat cross-legged in the center of the living room surrounded by six Sheikhs. In low and rapid rhythms they recited verses while spitting in my direction. I recognized some of the Sheikhs from my younger days at *dugsi* and prayed they hadn't remembered me.

My mother and father bore their eyes into me from the kitchen the entire time. I felt so low and worthless, consumed with shame and guilt. It was the most uncomfortable half hour of my life. When it was all said and done, my parents ordered me to pray two *rakaats* and beg *Allah* for His forgiveness.

From then on I was kept on what I like to call "suicide watch." My mother and father would make one of my siblings tail me whenever I went off upstairs. Bathroom visits were no longer normal and showers couldn't be more than ten minutes long. If I went to bed a few minutes earlier than usual my bedroom door would be cracked open. In would come my sister or brother and of course they always wanted to *talk*. "Were you crying," or "just be happy" became perfectly okay things to say to me.

I could never have a quiet moment to myself without someone barging in my room or thoughts. I envied my siblings for the freedom they could have alone and the non-invasive relationship they shared with our parents. At least they could *pee* in peace.

Three weeks have passed since then and things have hardly changed. My parents still look at me just a little too long and my siblings keep an eagle eye on me. Everyone will look my way when an antidepressant commercial comes on TV. Moments later, the channel will be changed to something more lighthearted like the news. I only wish they knew better than to treat my depression as a taboo. In my family the "d" word was equivalent to saying *Voldemort's* name. You must never dare speak it.

These days I can no longer speak freely about life and death without my mother shooting me a scary glare. The other day I said something along the lines of feeling like I were dead or close to it from the day's fiery heat. As a result my mother gave me the iciest stare in the entire world. I was positive that it was colder than any ice glacier in Antarctica. There were levels to my mother's glares and this one was off the scale mean.

Just last night my youngest sister Abla asked me if I was still "feeling down". At 17, she's four years my junior but the smartest person I'll ever know. As badly as I wanted to lie and say no, I felt the need to be real with her. She deserved to know how her older sister was really feeling. So I tried explaining it to her as best I could. I told her depression wasn't some dark cloud that would disappear with the rainy weather. It was something I had to deal with each and every day. I confessed that I was down but trying my best to push away all the dark thoughts and keep myself busy- in the hopes of keeping my mind busy too. She blinked a few times and muttered a sheepish "okay". In a matter of seconds, she turned back to whatever she was doing on her phone and stopped asking anymore questions. My friends' reactions weren't too ideal either.

A week ago I decided to come clean with them and share how bad I'd been feeling about myself. On the video call I mentioned getting, "depressive thoughts." Stupidly I made the mistake of using those same words in the hope they'd understand. Instead they admitted to getting them too and related it to listening to some songs from *Adele's* new album. Another one of my friends blamed it on being cooped indoors all day and suggested we, "do something exciting for once."

The straw that broke the camel's back was when my *Habaryar* Mulki came over for a visit. She had gotten back from a two week trip in Minnesota with gifts for everyone. I was in my room while she was doing the big giveaway. Suddenly, Abla rushed inside to tell me *Habaryar* Mulki wanted to see me. I reluctantly got up and went downstairs to go and see her. She was sitting on the armchair across from my mother and sisters, Bahja and Habsa.

When I went over to *Habaryar* she threw her arms around me and didn't let go for a good minute. With a shaking voice she told me how much she missed me. Not only that but how she dreamt of me. That was something I found particularly hard to believe. In the past *Habaryar* would always tell my mother how she never remembered her own dreams.

I just smiled when she said it, trying my best to appear cheerful. I knew my mom must have mentioned my depression to her since they had been so close. *Habaryar* later made me sit on the ground, just beside her feet. She handed me a sky high stack of new *batis*, dresses

50

and *abayas*. One look over at my sisters and they were already shooting darts at me with their eyes. They had only gotten two or three items each, while I received an entire new wardrobe. Just after *Habaryar* gave me the clothes, she threw her hands over her face dramatically and sighed.

Out loud she questioned why a girl as beautiful, intelligent and sweet as me would ever consider taking her own life. With eyes peeled to the ground, I said nothing. *Habaryar* went on mentioning how I used to be so happy and carefree when I was younger. Then she leaned towards me ever so slowly, and said I needed to live up to the meaning of my name, which ironically enough meant happy.

I almost lost it then and forced myself to hold back my laughter. I knew my *Habaryar* had good intentions but like everyone else she failed to understand something. I didn't choose to feel the way I did. Depression picked *me*.

It wasn't like I woke up every morning taking an oath to hate myself and cry all day and night. I wished they could understand that and stop placing all the blame on me. It wasn't like I didn't do that enough on my own already. The way I saw it, the depression was my own test. I saw it similar to how others were faced with food addiction or anger issues. Some days I couldn't help but wish that I were faced with some easier trial- something that didn't involve me considering my death on a near daily basis. For me, depression was much like a vicious tyrant. It oppressed my mind and enchained it. As a result, it seemed hopeless for me to ever be free and take control of myself. Every new day was it's own struggle, and I was unlucky enough to always be on the losing end.

While lying in bed after another pitiful crying session- I tried making sense of it all. Yes, what I was dealing with was very real and difficult. Yet that didn't mean I could allow myself to fall victim. Something in my heart was telling me that I was bigger than this, and that I was stronger than any kind of weakness depression could affect me with. I told myself that I had all the power to change my mind and how I perceived myself. I could stop feeling the way I did and be different, the one thing I always hoped for myself to become.

After a few long minutes of giving myself an inspirational, mountain moving pep talk, I fell asleep. The very next day I woke up feeling worse than the last. All I could think about was how worthless, pathetic and useless I was. I hated myself most for waking up and still being alive. So I tossed myself back into bed, cried and slept till late evening.

Some days were worse than others, but the feelings were just shades of the same color. I felt powerless to the crippling thoughts that ran through my mind. They made me so numb and the only defense I had against them was my tears. I often thought about the day when my eyes would eventually grow dry and I'd lose my ability to shed any more of them. I wasn't sure it was an actual possibility, but I couldn't help but think about it plenty.

With each new day, and rising of the sun, I was falling deeper into my own dark abyss. My depression was only growing worse with time. Abla and my parents were no doubt taking notice. I could hardly get myself out of bed in the morning, or find a reason to bother living for that matter. When I wasn't sulking in bed I was wandering aimlessly around the house, with what must have appeared as a look of defeat clouding my face.

There were moments I could feel *Hooyo's* worried gaze lingering over me. Outside of her stares she never bothered herself with taking the time to speak to me. *Aabo's* answer to my depression was trying to keep me as busy as possible throughout the day. He would often request me to do this or that chore and buy random things from the grocery store. It was always me and never any of my other siblings. As much as I hated the idea of going out I consistently forced myself to. A part of me believed it could help and maybe keep me distracted from my own feelings of worthlessness.

At some point in it all I began to question God. Why hadn't He been helping me and delivering me from my own self-destruction? Why had He filled me with all these ugly thoughts about myself? What made me so unlucky? Did He hate me? I didn't stop over thinking these things until I became obsessed. A part of me tried to tell myself that God had nothing to do with my misery. Maybe I had been the only cause of my pitifulness.

Admittedly, it was hard praying five times a day with a belief that God didn't care very much for me. I questioned why I had to be so obligated. I had always been taught that God wasn't in need of my worship of Him and that it was for my own salvation. It wasn't like I didn't want to pray to Him any longer. I just felt consumed with confusion as to why He wouldn't answer my cries of help.

There must have been a huge disconnect I told myself. Yet it wasn't like I was a bad Muslim, *I couldn't be.* I prayed consistently and stayed away from drugs, alcohol, partying and guys. So why wasn't God coming to my aid? What was so wrong with me that made me exempt from His help? Was there some evil deep down in my soul that I was unaware of?

These questions inspired me to make a change. My spirituality began to grow more and more important to me. My daily aim was to never go a day without reading *Quran*, praying on time and being in constant remembrance of God. Some days it helped me and on others it had no visible effect. I grew even more helpless as the ugly thoughts suffocated me. When would I see my way out of this? When was my happy ending going to come? The questions in my mind began to multiply over time. I would stay up in bed for hours asking myself things I didn't have the nerve to answer.

The fact was I hated my depression. All I could do was over think to the point of complete exhaustion. I had no time for anything else because my mind was keeping me so preoccupied. The things I told myself began to grow much darker over time. *I deserve to have every bone in my body broken. Why couldn't I fall victim to some terminal illness and eventually die? Why couldn't my insides erupt?*

I was so worthless and pitiful in my mind. Nothing could convince me otherwise. I began to isolate myself from family and friends more. I would spend countless days and nights in bed or sitting by my window. My parents and siblings occasionally came in at noon and sometimes in the evening to check up on me. I convinced myself that they were checking to see if I were still alive. It was clear they still thought I had suicidal tendencies. The truth was I wanted death. I dreamed of that escape but I just couldn't bring myself to do it. That reality could only make me feel much worse about myself.

I told myself that I valued my life more but that didn't seem like a good enough answer. If I cared so much why didn't I live my life happily? I had some active choice in it all. Or maybe I feared God enough to not meet him by my own will. In that I admittedly felt better about myself. At least questioning God hadn't made me lose my fear of Him.

****

That Wednesday afternoon I went downstairs craving a citrus drink. Usually I would get these cravings and have an immediate need to fill them. Months ago, I got the same craving and borrowed my mom's van and drove to the nearest convenience store with Abla. At almost two am we dashed inside to grab two mango drinks and hot chips. At the time I only had my driver's permit, but I didn't let that stop me from answering the call of citrus.

I knew there would be some fresh squeezed orange juice from a day ago, but there was fruit punch too. Without a doubt I was choosing the second. There was something about artificially flavored drinks that filled my heart with happiness. With this in mind I sped down the stairs but stopped myself midway. It was then I recognized the voice of my neighbor and immediately froze on the step I stood on. She was a relative of my mother's purely through tribe with no real relation to me. And yet I still called her auntie out of respect. She wasn't the nicest woman you could meet. Whenever she came to visit my mother she would only spread gossip and rumors. I categorized her as the type to talk about other people's children while ignoring her own. She was my mother's age but didn't share her sense of class.

I knew it was too late to backtrack and go back upstairs. Besides, I was no coward and this was my own home. I would go downstairs to get my drink and go back up when I felt like it. I didn't care that there was a visitor, although that had stopped me many times before. Taking a deep breath I found the courage in me to greet her like my mother had always forced me to. Pulling on the fakest big smile I extended my hand out to her.

"*Assalamu allaykum habaryar. Sidee tahay?*" I said in an overly chipper tone. She'd seen me countless times in public and I never seemed to greet her so kindly before.

"*Wa alaykum assalam habaryar. Fiican, se tahay?*" She half smiled, while looking me up and down. For a moment I thought I were half naked from the look she was giving me. It was then I realized I hadn't been wearing a *garbasaar* and sported just a hoodie over my too-short-for-me *baati*. It was one of my old favorites that shrank in the washer weeks ago.

Standing there awkwardly I smiled uncomfortably. It wasn't even safe to wear what I wanted in the comfort of my own home. There was a lot of nerve in this woman that I couldn't just look past. I wasn't sure how *Hooyo* tolerated her company at all.

"*Alhamdulilah.*" I replied while speeding towards the kitchen. Once safe I pulled the hoodie over my head as I rolled my eyes. *Hooyo* was going to grill me about not staying around longer and asking about her family. I just knew she would. I opened the dishwasher and grabbed a glass cup. After setting the cup on the table I opened up the fridge and searched for my beloved fruit juice. A few minutes of looking I decided to give up and slowly turned around towards the trash bin. The carton was there just next to a dripping can of oily tuna.

I sighed and settled for the container of squeezed orange juice instead. There were bits of pulp in it that would force me to swallow and chew all at the same time. *Hooyo* didn't believe in removing the pulp from

55

orange juice and made my siblings and I keep it inside whenever we were juicing.

Once I finished drinking I rinsed the glass and left it to sit in the sink. Now I could escape upstairs I told myself. All I needed to do was walk as quickly past *Hooyo* as humanly possible. As soon as I entered the living room I ducked my head, and began speed walking. Evidently I wasn't going fast enough because *Hooyo* caught me just in time.

"Haniya!" My mother cried out. "*Kaale*. Go and make us some *shaah*."

I sighed, and trotted back towards the kitchen.

Serving tea to guests was a Somali custom that I despised for the life of me. Our guests could pop in anytime; day or night, and *Hooyo* would expect fresh tea to be made for them. It didn't matter that it was ten p.m. on a weekday, or ten a.m. on a sleepy weekend. I hated doing it but knew better than to argue with *Hooyo*. First I poured hot water into the kettle that was fortunately clean for once. Next, I grabbed the cinnamon, cardamom and cloves from the cabinet. I grabbed bits of each and threw a mix of them into the mortar. There I was on the kitchen floor pounding at the bits while the neighbor's voice interrupted my quiet.

From where I was sitting I could hear some of their conversation more clearly now.

"But she's not the most beautiful woman in town! She'd do good to control that mouth of hers before he goes hunting for another wife. This city is full of young, beautiful and educated women. What's she compared to any of them?"

I shook my head disgusted by what I was hearing. This was the respected guest I had to go out of my way for and serve. More than anything I wished to interject in the conversation, or for *Hooyo* to simply make her leave. Neither of those would be happening in my lifetime so I kept my opinions to myself.

"I just don't understand her. Why go ruining a good thing? She'll never find another man like him. Most men his age are losers getting high off *khat*. So what if he has a *Facebook* account? Why is that any of her business? She's out of line!" My mother added.

I felt annoyed at *Hooyo* for entertaining the gossip instead of ending it. It wasn't worth all the *dambi* to be talking crap about a random person. Aside from that, it just wasn't a very nice thing to do. I tried drowning out all the things I was hearing by humming to myself. That proved to be hard because of the volume at which they were speaking. Despite *Hooyo* and the neighbor being a few inches apart, they still felt the need to shout at one another.

Once I finished mashing up the ingredients for the tea, I got up to add them to the teapot. After a few minutes I added a cup of sugar and two tea bags. That's when I began to notice the wind shaking the trees outside. The kitchen window was open to our backyard and adjacent to a large orange tree we had. The wind was softly jostling the branches side to side, in a mesmerizing rhythm. I found myself lost in a moment of childhood nostalgia, of days running around the tree and attempting to climb it.

Hooyo woke me up from my trance.

"Haniya! *Naa kaale! Soo orod!*" She said aloud. I could hear the neighbor whispering something to her, but couldn't understand what that was.

"*Haye Hooyo!* I'm coming!" I replied as I lowered the flame from the range and rushed into the living room.

Hooyo and the neighbor both turned to me at once. I felt a little anxious all of a sudden and wondered what they were going to say. The neighbor had a strange smirk over her face.

"Haniya, what was the name of the girl who got expelled from your high school? I forget."

"Umm..Layla Hersi?" I answered feeling a little unsure of myself. There was something very intimidating about being put on the spot in front of your neighbor and mother.

Hooyo nodded and turned to the neighbor as if to say she had been right all along.

The neighbor chuckled. "I suppose the whole family inherited the crazy gene."

I turned to my mother confused, seeking some type of explanation. She said nothing.

"I always just thought it was her mother, but it definitely hit the kids as well."

"I knew she was crazy from the very first time I met her. Everyone else just thought she had a bad temper but I knew even then. She should go admit herself somewhere." The neighbor remarked as my mother erupted in loud laughter.

I just stood there almost waiting to be excused by *Hooyo*, but was ignored instead.

"Admit herself where?" *Hooyo* asked hooting with laughter. She hadn't been able to contain herself.

"You know what they used to do with the insane back in Somalia. They would tie them by the leg to a tree or pole. At least here they're nice enough to put them in a house with some nurses. They're living in luxury those people, and all of them are nuts!"

Hooyo clapped her hand against her leg while the neighbor went on and on about the living conditions of the mentally insane in the country. I felt sick to my stomach and finally got the message to disappear. I retreated into the kitchen to the whistling teapot, and shut off the stove. My thoughts were running wild, and I felt a stinging pang of hurt in my chest. I couldn't contain the tears that fell from my face as my body began to shake with emotion.

Sobbing I replayed my mother's laughter and the disgusting comments made against the mentally insane. Everything in their words triggered me into feeling a deep sense of hurt and anxiety. They were in no way speaking about me, but I felt every bit offended. If that was how they spoke about the mentally ill they would think just as badly about the depressed.

I felt betrayed by my mother and her lack of compassion. I couldn't bring myself to serve them even though I knew I had to. With quickness I wiped at my eyes and dabbed cold water over my face in the sink. Then I grabbed the serving tray from the cabinet nearest to the stove. After pouring two cups of tea, another for milk, and a last for sugar I placed them all there.

I took a deep breath, putting on a brave face, and set back out into the danger zone. My mother and the neighbor were speaking in low whispers now, and I didn't care to hear a word of it. Very carefully I set the tray in front of them on the coffee table and went back upstairs.

"Haniya, where are the sweets?" *Hooyo* asked with a bit of annoyance in her voice.

I sighed. "Isn't the tea sweet enough?"

The neighbor laughed. "Kids these days are nothing but disrespectful. Why talk back to your mother? Go and do as she asks. Back in Somalia we wouldn't tolerate such behavior. It's only..."

"Haniya go and get the cookies, while the tea is still hot." *Hooyo* barked with clenched teeth.

I sighed and went back into the kitchen. Doing as I was told, I grabbed the bag of *buskuud* over the fridge. I shuffled my feet back into the living room and set the bag alongside the tea.

"That wasn't so hard now, was it?" *Hooyo* asked in a mocking manner. I barely managed to meet her angry eyes and felt ashamed of myself all of a sudden. I hadn't meant to embarrass her, but I couldn't help but feel frustrated with her and her "guest."

"Sorry *Hooyo*." I said lowly, before treading back upstairs. *Hooyo* said nothing and began pouring the tea. I looked back around to see the neighbor filling her mouth with a star shaped cookie. I hated every bit of that woman and wished *Hooyo* wouldn't have her at our house. Everything about her demeanor was nasty, even her eating habits. I didn't linger and went off upstairs to my room. Abla was still in the shower and that gave me the time I needed to break down and cry.

Laying my head over my pillow, I curled up like a child and began sobbing.

It was as if all the light was gone from the world and nothing but darkness surrounded me. I kept replaying what they said and the way in which they laughed. My illness was a joke to them. I would never be able to confront *Hooyo* about how I was feeling. She wouldn't take me serious and would just laugh in my face.

60

I couldn't stop the tears from falling as a headache began to overcome me. My eyes began to grow sore from all the tears and my body was shaking. I hadn't broken down like this is in days and *oh how easily* I could crumble. Moments like these left me torn and vulnerable. All I could manage to do after these times was lie in bed broken and weak. The sound of dripping water all but stopped in the bathroom and I guessed that Abla would be out soon. I tried wiping my face but the tears wouldn't stop falling.

****

Later that same day Abla came into my room to tell me *Hooyo* wanted to see me.

It may or may not have been about what happened earlier, but I wasn't entirely sure.

"Is she mad?" I asked Abla, the words scraping against my tongue.

"I don't know. I can never tell with *Hooyo*." Abla replied, not looking up from her cell phone.

I sighed and pulled away the comfortable covers of my bed. Abla was right about *Hooyo*. She wore her poker face very well and most days you couldn't guess her mood.

If it had been about earlier I told myself I'd try and remain calm. I could tell she was upset with me earlier, and it only made sense for her to speak to me about it now. Without giving it another thought I rushed downstairs and made my way to the living room. *Hooyo* was applying homemade henna on her hands from a wooden bowl, with her feet propped up against the coffee table.

"*Haa Hooyo, maxaa rabtay?*" I said it in the sweetest voice I could muster. There was a long silence in the room after I said the words that made my skin grow cold.

61

"*Nayaa maxaa kugu dhacay?* What's the matter with you? Why are you disrespecting me in front of Khadra? Why can't you learn to keep your mouth shut and just listen? Don't you have any sense in you?!" She exclaimed, glaring deep into me with every breath.

I sighed, of course it would be about earlier. I didn't know why I entertained the thought of it not being. *Hooyo* shuffled around, sitting upright, and narrowed her eyes at me.

"Answer me *nayaa*. What's wrong with you?"

"Nothing's wrong with me and I won't do it again. Happy?"

Hooyo raised her eyebrow, laughing heartily. "*Haye*, you want to act that way with me, *miyaa?*"

"*Hooyo* why do you even bother keeping her around? She's not a nice person at all", I complained totally out of line. I knew I was playing with fire, but I didn't care to get burned.

"Is that any of your business girl? Look how far you've gone now! Are you not hearing yourself?!" *Hooyo* was one minute away from getting up and giving me a beating. I hadn't grown too old for those, and she would be more than happy to remind me of that.

"I am *Hooyo*. I just don't understand. She's a horrible person and doesn't do anything but bad mouth other people. That's only a waste of time and *dambi*." I said speaking with passion.

Hooyo shook her head. "Never in my life did I believe my own child would tell me who I could and could not speak to. *Ilaahayoow*, what have I done to deserve this girl's disrespect?"

I drew nearer to her, "*Hooyo* I'm only telling the truth. Who's to say she won't speak badly about you one day?"

The next thing I knew the remote was flying in the air and headed right for me. I quickly dodged it in time and caught my breath. "What are you doing?!"

"Something I should have done sooner! You're all spoiled. Khadra was right about you American kids. All spoiled and ungrateful, only days away from betraying your trust!" *Hooyo* complained shouting.

I sighed. "She only says that because it's her truth. Her own children have been out doing things you would never believe. She can't paint me with the same brush because of them!"

"What would you know about her kids? They're all good and well-mannered. None of them would have the nerve to speak to me the way you are if I was their mother! Besides they haven't tried killing themselves from what I know either!" *Hooyo* exclaimed.

I lowered my head, and scoffed. "Yes, well that's good for them. They should consider themselves lucky for not being depressed like I am!"

"Why do you keep going on about this depression? It doesn't exist and never will. That's all one big lie to get people to buy medications they don't need. Depression isn't real and you would do well to remember that now."

Tears began to shoot out from my eyes, but I didn't bother with wiping them.

"No *Hooyo*, you would do well to realize that it is. Your own daughter is suffering from it every day and you have no idea! I'm sorry I make you feel so ashamed!" I screamed, my voice falling with a cry.

I ran upstairs, and headed directly for my room. *Hooyo's* sudden silence was beating against the walls at full volume. I knew her words would stay with me forever.

As I slammed the door, Abla turned and gave me her full attention.

"Hey, I heard some of that. Are you okay?"

I ignored her as I buried my body underneath my blanket, tears and boogers running down my face at once. If ever a moment to harm myself, now would be the best one. Abla didn't quiet down.

"She said some messed up things I know, but she didn't mean it. It's just her anger."

I tore my hot blanket away from my face.

"Yes she did! She's never been more embarrassed of me since that day. She can't even speak to me without looking at me with disgust."

Abla sighed exasperated. "I'm sorry she said all of that to you. It's not true. Depression is real and so are your feelings. She just doesn't understand."

"I really don't want to talk now Abla, but thanks for your concern." I said clenching my hands together.

Abla fell silent, and then I heard her silently get up and close the door behind her a moment later. She was always considerate of my feelings.

As much as I wanted to lie there and keep crying I knew I would have to pray in no less than twenty minutes. *Asr* was just around the corner and I didn't want to intentionally miss it by not getting up out of bed. In a way I was thankful for the prayers. No matter how bad I was feeling they made me get up out of bed and shift my focus away from my emotions.

Allah entered my mind, and a short moment of calm fell over me. The reality of Him watching over me in that very moment hit me.

Everything that just happened was decreed and I was a part of that. "Not a leaf falls but He knows it." He was well-aware of what I was feeling and knew that it was real and existing. I shut my eyes and imagined myself in prayer already.

As I knelt down for *sujood* , I asked Him to take away all the anxiety and depression. I begged and pleaded for His help and peace. I craved the peace He could bring me from the rainstorm I was forced to endure each new day. *Allah* was waiting for me to speak to Him again.

I slowly rose out of bed and took a deep long breath. I planned to offer my prayers and supplicate longer than I ever had. I would pour my heart into my prayers and ask for His help. I wanted Him to listen.

****

Some weeks had passed before I finally got around to making any plans with my friends.

We would go see a movie at seven and have dinner at Vista. The girls and I had been going back and forth in a group text all week deciding on a good day for us to hang out. This Friday just happened to be the best time for us. Some of us were going to carpool and chip in for gas money. I happened to be amongst that group and that meant I'd have to be ready earlier.

Sometime around four I finally decided to get myself ready and pick out an outfit. I was the polar opposite of my younger sister Abla who would have an outfit in mind days ahead. She'd leave whatever she was going to wear in the front of her wardrobe and lay out the accessories to go along with it. I'd never been as organized as her and consistently settled for doing things at the very last minute.

I stood akimbo in front of my closet as my eyes wandered indecisively over what to wear. There was a lot to choose from, but it wasn't like time was on my side. So I went for one of my more basic outfits. I'd wear a black maxi dress, olive bomber jacket and black chiffon shawl. A bracelet and ring or two could be thrown in as well.

Just as I got ready to start undressing there was a knock at the door. Perfect timing.

"Come in." I said, while keeping my eyes locked ahead. Abla wouldn't knock so that meant someone else was standing on the other side. I wondered who it could be.

It was *Hooyo* who had come in, wearing a loose fitting purple *baati* and matching satin *masr* over her head. She looked tired as usual but also alert in a strange way. I moved away from my closet then. Things had been pretty quiet between the two of us since the big fight. We both tried staying out of each other's way as best we could.

"*Haye*. Where are you going?" She asked her eyes meeting mine.

"Out with my friends. I think Abla mentioned it to you." I reminded her with a feeling of uneasiness filling my gut. Something felt so off in that moment. There was a vibe I was getting and I didn't like it one bit.

"*Haa*, I remember now. Are you leaving right this minute?" She asked while taking a seat at the edge of my bed. She stroked the velvety blanket and patted the space next to her.

"Sit, we need to talk." She said in a tone I wasn't used to hearing. I looked for some kind of clue or hint as to what *Hooyo* wanted to talk about. There was nothing in her face for me to read.

With slow hesitant steps, I inched towards the bed and sat beside her. Head bent and legs crossed, I waited to hear the big talk she had prepared. I had never seen my *Hooyo* appear so solemn in my life. It was so unsettling.

66

"Abla is worried about you. I don't think she's convinced you're getting any better. She's been speaking to me and we both think its best you get help."

"Help?" I asked my hands growing limp all of a sudden. What had she meant by getting *help*?

"Yes, professional. How would you feel about going to a therapist? The insurance won't cover it but I think we can make it work on our own." *Hooyo* said.

I was hardly able to process the words *Hooyo* had just spoken.

"You don't have to say yes now but think about it. It's always open to you." She said reaching to grasp my hand. I didn't pull my hand away and squeezed hers softly.

There was a sweet warmth emanating from her touch that forced tears from my eyes. I hadn't felt my mother's touch in so long and I suddenly became needy for her affection.

"We haven't forgotten about you. None of us have. Especially me, I worry all the time."

I smiled and wiped at my eyes, embarrassed. "You never said anything."

Hooyo sighed, "I never needed to. Haniya, I shouldn't have said those things to you that day. I can't make you not feel something that you do. It's out of my control."

"I'm sorry too, *Hooyo*. For not doing as you said when Khadra came and speaking back to you."

Hooyo waved her hand dismissively. "I forgot all about that now. You've already been forgiven."

I smiled, and pulled my arms around her and felt a huge weight fall off my shoulders.

I began to feel an overwhelming sense of awe. I thought of the *Quranic* verse, "*Verily after hardship comes ease.*" I'd been a witness to that truth. Of all people I would have never expected *Hooyo* to understand my depression. She held me tighter now, and for once I let the idea cross my mind. I had a real chance of defeating this thing. I had my family by my side and *Allah* always watching over me. I was never meant to lose.

Case No. 23

The only thing that felt right on nights like these was spicy lentil soup, so that was what I ordered. Too bad it was still too hot to eat.

Growing impatient, I shifted my eyes towards the window. My stomach growled as raindrops danced down the windowsill. So typical of my Seattle. Rainy and cold nights were no stranger to this city. My phone beeped and drew my attention back to the table.

I reached over to pick it up only to see it was a message from my phone company. *How disappointing,* I thought, expecting it to be a text from one of my friends. I knew we'd lost touch over the past few months, but I still wouldn't count it out. If I hadn't forgotten about them what would make them forget about me? At least that's what I tried telling myself.

I turned my attention back to the soup. In one quick motion, I lifted the silver spoon from the folded napkin, and dove it into the bowl. The steam was still rising and I knew the heat would scorch my tongue as I ate. I wouldn't take any chances this time, so I blew softly trying to prevent myself from another accident.

Delicious, as always.

I lowered the spoon back into the soup and scooped up some more. I stopped every now and then to take a sip of cold water. The soup was pretty spicy, even for someone with a high tolerance for it like myself. Each bit packed a one two punch that left my tongue searing in pain, and yet I couldn't stop myself from coming back for more. As I ate, I let my eyes wander around the odd little diner. It was a hole in the wall place just a few blocks from my house. During the spring semester I'd seen people coming down these streets carrying their coffees and takeout trays. I guessed there to have been some kind of popular cafe around. Then one day while walking in the area I tried it out for myself.

At first, I wasn't too impressed by the look or size of it. The walls were completely white with no decorations, not even a single cheap painting hung on them. The worst part was the tables that were a tattered green. Nothing seemed too appealing about the restaurant for me at all, until I ordered it from the menu. From the very moment I tried the spicy lentil soup I was hooked.

I leaned over to finish the rest of my soup, sending another spicy spoonful into my mouth.

Another beep.

I flung the spoon back into the bowl and turned my eyes to my phone, wondering if it was urgent. It was another text. My interest peaked but that went away as soon as I saw the sender:

Abti Haybe.

He sent me an address and said I needed to be there in ten minutes tops. I studied the street name and realized I wasn't too far away. South Side. I could get there in half the time. I set my phone down and finished the rest of my soup.

****

The rain had begun to ease up once I hit the road. The only trace of it left were the sprinkles on my windshield and even those were beginning to fade. The streets were nearly empty even though it was only nine pm. I kept at a steady pace.

I didn't want to keep *Abti* Haybe waiting. He wasn't the most patient man in the world, and being late would only trigger his infamous bad temper. Plus I knew it would only reflect negatively on him if I were. I used my windshield wipers now as it began to lightly sprinkle.

I was 17 when I first accompanied my uncle on an exorcism.

Nothing could prepare me for seeing what I had that night. I'll never forget the way in which that woman's body shook or the deep haunting voice that drawled out of her. All the hairs on my neck and arms rose when she twisted her lips into a deranged smile at me. I still ask myself why I didn't just run when she lunged at me. My feet didn't seem to want to move. I had only realized the true threat I was facing when it took five whole men to restrain her.

I guess something changed in me that night. The world of the unseen had become apparent to me, and all I could do was stare in awe. I knew from that point on that I needed to see more. It didn't matter to me what my friends or parents had to say about it. Their worries and warnings meant little to me. *Abti* Haybe himself couldn't convince me otherwise. I tagged along with him at any given chance, and witnessed all the things I could no longer deny seeing.

At first, everyone was worried for me. They couldn't make sense of my newfound interest. What would possess me to want to be around the possessed? There were times I asked myself the same question. I never really found an answer.

I just knew it was something I wanted to be a part of. There was no denying that it was strange, but nobody could complain if I wasn't getting into any real trouble. Besides, I had been with my *Abti* Haybe; a strong, smart, and well respected man in my family and all of the community.

He was a religious man as well, who finished reading the *Quran* a score of times throughout his six decades. At the age of twenty-six, he began to use his recitation to help others by casting out evil spirits

71

from their bodies. It was only after my fifth exorcism that I became a real help to my uncle. Alongside other men, I found myself holding and restraining the possessed person as they punched and kicked into mid-air.

Abti Haybe was as surprised as I was with my sudden action, but he didn't shun me for what I did. I could feel myself grow more close to *Abti* in those moments than ever before. There was a level of trust he instilled in me that I promised myself I would never take for granted. From that point on I became an assistant of sorts to *Abti* Haybe. I would carry his *musxaf* along with his water, and oils that had *Quran* recited over them. I'd be the first one to restrain and hold down the possessed if need be. I would go off into another room to speak to the family members of the possessed and ask them a series of typical questions.

Things like, "what kind of unusual behavior have you noticed?" Or, "do they get up and walk about constantly", and "are they feeling depressed and angry often?" Five years later, and all of these very same things are asked. Only now I can drive up to the home of the possessed instead of tagging along with my uncle in his jeep.

During the weekdays I did my best to keep up with schoolwork, and on weekends the spirits held my complete attention. There was no denying it was a lot different from what other twenty-two years olds may have done in their spare time. I knew it was hard for my friends to understand. In the past I'd reject their invites to hang out and play basketball. Now they didn't even bother calling my line anymore. It felt like they gave up on me.

Some days I woke up telling myself the exorcisms weren't worth standing in the way of my childhood friendships. Then I reminded myself how regular not hanging out became for me. It wouldn't be very hard for me to picture myself zoning out mid-conversation or taking too long to get a joke. I told myself it wasn't worth the awkwardness that would most likely ensue.

Every now and then I grow lonely. Being in the company of my uncle didn't prove to be very fulfilling. I got depressed a lot too.

I tried to stop thinking so much about it and stay focused on driving.

My GPS told me I was only one mile off now. I began to grow a little restless; like I did each time I made these drives. Fear wasn't a factor with me in these exorcisms. It was more like an overwhelming itching sensation that settled once I saw the possessed. People always said there was a good chance of *Abti* Haybe getting possessed and myself as well. Fortunately that had never happened as of yet. There were certain measures that *Abti* Haybe and I took with these exorcisms.

For instance, we never told the *jinn* our first and last names, or the names of our family members. Our personal information and affiliations with others was a no-go subject in each of our exorcisms. We did well to never cross any lines while conversing with the possessed, knowing what kind of danger we'd be putting ourselves through otherwise. *Abti* Haybe always reminded me to never show my vulnerability or fear. He said the evil spirits could sniff it out like fresh blood in a forest. If they knew you were afraid that would increase your own chances of becoming possessed. *Abti* Haybe always took charge during the possessions, and when he could sense my fear, he no longer requested my help.

There were times I had become so shaken by what I'd seen. Backing away from the possessed and leaving rooms used to be my norm. *Abti* Haybe would wait till after a session, and then ask me if I wanted out. Each time I would tell him that I was completely invested and not willing to quit. *Abti* Haybe would believe me and take my word for truth.

73

During one exorcism months ago I had suddenly grown nauseous. A feeling of twisted knots began to overwhelm my stomach. The possessed man we were visiting hadn't showered in weeks. The *jinn* inside of him was irrationally afraid to bathe in water and influenced the man to ignore his own personal hygiene. Funky smelling fumes filled the man's home as a result and left many in that house swaying in discomfort and disgust.

Abti Haybe didn't flinch one bit and seemed indifferent to the repulsive smell.

I remember clutching my shirt over my nose to block out the odor. *Abti* Haybe noticed this and pulled me aside to the other end of the room. The possessed man turned his attention to us and began shuffling in his seat manically. The wife of the man began to look concerned as well and began whispering to a man in the room. She looked doubtful.

"If you're feeling offended you can go on home." He said it in a calm manner.

I shook my head, protesting. "No-no *Abti*. Trust me I can handle it."

Abti grabbed a hold of my arm all of a sudden. "Okay. So pull your shirt away from your nose and start paying attention. His family is here, show some respect."

"*Haye, Abti*." I replied as I removed my shirt from my nose. He had a point.

I wasn't as attentive as I should have been. The smell drew away all my focus. As much as I wanted to run outside for a fresh breath of air I stayed put. I hung around and helped *Abti* Haybe with whatever needed to be done for the possessed.

We had been successful in casting the *jinn* from the man's body that day. I doubt it would have been the case if I hadn't forced myself to ignore the nauseating smell. Abti was a wise man.

****

The rain was pouring harder as I found parking along the street. I would wait a few minutes until it settled down and then head inside. I checked the address on my phone again for the house number. 4331. Something about this area seemed so familiar to me. I sifted through my memories to try and figure out the connection but there was none. It wasn't such a bad thing that I didn't know the possessed person, anyway. *Abti* Haybe said this was a job that was best left for the reserved. According to him it wasn't an asset to know the possessed person for fear they may speak badly about you or act erratically. I was a man of few friends, much like my *Abti*, but every now and then I would come across a familiar face.

Luckily, that wouldn't be the case for me this time around. I forced the keys out of the ignition and got out of my car. I pulled the collar of my jacket over my ears and sped towards the other end of the street. I'd only been out for a few seconds but was almost nearly soaked through. I was only a few minutes late, but *Abti* Haybe would still grill me about it. As usual, I'd have to apologize over and over, making promises to be more punctual in the future.

When I reached the home I realized I forgot to bring the water and oils in the back of my car. I told myself it was okay since *Abti* always carried around a few of his own water bottles and oils. If anything I was the muscle for *Abti*, seeing as to how much older he was getting. With this reasoning I justified leaving the things in the car and went up to the house, knocking twice.

There was a mat outside the door and I used it to dry my shoes. *Abti* was very strict about coming to a person's home with clean clothes and shoes. Even though I would be taking off my shoes as soon as I got in, he still felt it to be an important habit to keep. So I dried my *Addidas* against the emerald green carpet and knocked again.

Abti advised me against using the doorbell, for fear of disturbing the families and alarming the possessed. It didn't matter how long you had to wait, it was better knocking then ringing, he would remind me.

I heard footsteps on the other side of the door and stopped wiping my shoes. An older woman with glasses answered and smiled kindly at me.

"Assalamu Alaykum, soo dhaaf habaryar," she said, making room for me to pass.

"Wa alaykum assalam habaryar." I replied making my way into the warmth of the home.

As usual, the first thing I noticed was the strong smell of incense filling the air.

The house was larger inside than it looked outdoors, which was another thing I took note of on these encounters. I waited for the older woman and smiled as she led me into the living room. I could see the side of *Abti* Haybe's beard and *kufi*, as well as two other men seated with him. The woman wearing glasses stopped all of a sudden and turned back around towards me.

"You're Shamsa's boy, aren't you?" She tilted her head to the side. I nodded smiling.

"Haa, habaryar. Yes, I am. Her youngest." I took a moment to look around the house.

"I wasn't entirely sure but had an idea you could be. All of her boys look so much like her. My son went to school with you, I believe. Do you remember Mahad?"

76

I thought on it. Mahad? The name didn't immediately ring a bell. She must have confused me for one of my brothers, of which there were six. We all shared similar features, as well as height, so it could have been a possibility.

"*Maya habaryar*, but maybe it was one of my brothers."

She nodded. "Yes, you may be right, but you look about his age. Anyway, you should go join them. Let me not distract you with all this talk. May *Allah* reward you for your work *habaryar*."

"*Ameen in sha Allah*, and thank you." I told her before walking into the living room.

Abti turned to look at me, and then quickly turned away. He was conversing with two other men, as he held a cup of tea in his right hand. I knew he must have been annoyed.

"*Assalamu alaykum*," I said aloud, as I went up to shake the two men's hands whom I had never seen before. They returned my *salaam* and shook my hand happily. I joined them and sat on the floor.

"This is my nephew, Loyan. My younger sister Shamsa's boy." Abti said, nodding towards me.

"Nice to meet you all." I said as the men both turned their attention to me and nodded.

"He'll be helping me today. He's a smart boy so you need not worry." *Abti* added not smiling. I lowered my head respectfully and waited for either of the men to speak.

"My name's Aden Ugaas, and this is my younger brother Husni," the older of the two men said.

He was more heavy set, with a lighter complexion and thick mustache. His brother was darker, thinner, but much younger looking. I studied Aden's face, trying to guess where I'd seen him before.

"That must have been my wife who you just spoke to now." His eyes darted towards the kitchen area.

I smiled again, and nodded. "Yes, we just spoke."

"Would you like some tea?" Husni asked, while pointing towards the tray set with cups, tea, milk, sugar, biscuits, and *xalwo*. It was the typical welcome for most of the homes we'd been to.

"Yes that would be nice, thank you." I said while pouring myself a cup. Afterwards, I added a bit of milk and placed two biscuits on a small plate. Husni nodded approvingly, and then turned back towards *Abti*, seeking to continue whatever conversation they were having.

"Yes, this is a bit trickier than evil eye or your average possession. From what you both told me, it seems to me that someone has placed *sihr* upon him. It'll be more challenging to cast the *jinn* out, because the spell must first be broken. Do you have any clue as to who may have done it or wished him any ill?" Abti asked, turning to the brothers. They both exchanged a thoughtful look between themselves and shrugged helplessly.

"Everyone who knows him loves him." Aden said, who I guessed must have been the boy's father.

Husni nodded. "Yes, it's true. Every person who knows him has nothing but respect and admiration for him."

Abti stroked his beard, which was scattered with graying hairs. "Well, that's an interesting thing. You should understand, though, that not

78

everyone who seems like a friend may have good intentions. Was your boy very trusting of others? Did he know a lot of people?"

"Yes, he has many friends. Mahad has always been a popular young man," Aden answered.

Mahad. I heard the name again, but still nothing came to mind.

"So you're saying he had an enemy within his friend group?" Husni asked squinting his eyes and crossing his arms.

Abti nodded, "Yes, exactly."

Aden turned towards his brother, sharing a look of confusion. "But that's not possible."

"Anything is possible, brothers. Did you ever imagine he would be inflicted with a *jinn*?" *Abti* asked them.

Husni cleared his throat and answered for the both of them. "No, never."

I took slow sips at my tea, and broke off a bit of the biscuit nearest to me. It was shortbread.

"Try keeping your minds open to anything. I've been doing this work for several years and each case is different. Many people have experienced what you have and drawn conclusions about their loved ones that seemed impossible," *Abti* told them, looping his finger around the tea cup.

I nodded, and looked at the brothers for understanding. Husni was looking down thinking while Aden seemed to looked confused and frustrated.

"I see what you mean, but he's always been admired by people. No one could think to do him any harm," Aden argued.

"You know how much people respect him at school and the *masjid*. He's always been a mentor to the young boys there. They all look up to him." Aden turned to his brother for agreement. I tried thinking of what *masjid* that could be and asked myself if I had seen or heard of a Mahad at any of them. I only ever frequented two *masjids* that were a few miles from my home but couldn't remember anyone named Mahad that went there. I sipped at my tea some more.

"That's right, but we should keep our minds open. It's true. Someone you think of as a friend may very well see you as their enemy. It's the way of the world. Humans are imperfect creatures," Husni added wisely.

Abti interjected. "You're correct brother. That is precisely what I mean. Mahad may have taken the person as a friend, but in the other's eye he could have been the worst kind of enemy. I suggest you keep your minds open and ask around. I'd like to see the boy now, if you don't mind."

Aden and Husni shot up in a hurry. "Okay, we'll be sure to and we'll go get him now."

As they disappeared down the hall, *Abti* finished off the rest of his tea. I set my cup down and wiped my hands against the front of my jeans. That feeling of anxiety was building up in me again. This time it was triggered by a strange curiosity to see the possessed. Who was the man of my *twenty-third case?*

"You're late, again," *Abti* said, banging his cup against the tray. He wiped his mouth and turned to me for an explanation. I could have sworn this very same moment had occurred four other times in the past.

80

"I know. Sorry *Abti*," I replied, for the hundredth time that year.

He shook his head. "A man who isn't on time doesn't earn the respect of others," *Abti* said, while looking ahead.

I moved the tray aside and stretched my legs. *Abti* shot me a strange look and snapped his fingers.

"What are you doing? Is this your home or are you a relative to these people?"

I quickly folded my legs back together and unzipped my jacket. *Abti* shook his head again. He was always quick to scold me or teach me a lesson. Sometimes I felt like he took to speaking to me like a child he was forced to raise, now that all his kids were married.

All of a sudden Aden and Husni reappeared, this time with Mahad.

He towered over them, with broad shoulders and a thick mop of dark curly hair. He shared the same complexion as Husni and looked less like Aden. Maybe I mixed up who had been his father after all. The brothers held tightly onto each side of his waist and arms, as the man trudged across the room. From a distance, I couldn't tell anything was wrong with him. It was only when he drew nearer to me that I saw his wild bulging eyes and dazed look across his face. He sat down with the men and then shot back up. They held him down again and looped their arms tightly around him.

Abti looked closely at Mahad. All of a sudden, *Abti* turned towards me and asked,

"Have you brought the things with you?"

I froze, and then looked at *Abti*, and then back at the brothers.

"Yes, they're in the car. I'll go get them now," I replied with a flash of embarrassment.

Abti sighed. "Well go and hurry. You should have done it earlier."

"I know…," I muttered under my breath. He was right. I should have retrieved them when I had a chance. Aden looked a little annoyed and then turned to *Abti*.

"This is Mahad. My oldest boy."

I got up slowly and looked at him. *Abti* held out his hand but Mahad didn't take it. He just kept looking around fearfully, like he'd been taken to some awful place.

"Go on then and hurry," *Abti* ordered, noticing me lingering. I nodded and went off to get the things from the car. As I walked through the living room I saw a banner with a cardinal on it and couldn't help but stare. The year 2012 was written over the bird in bright red letters. *Hoover High School.*

I turned back around to *Abti* who was speaking with the brothers as they struggled to hold down a much physically stronger Mahad. Just how could I have forgotten him? I took a deep breath and slid into my sneakers.

For two whole years that very same person had made my life a living hell, mercilessly bullying me to no end. He was a cousin of one of my friends and just so happened to despise my existence.

I made my way outside in the cold rain and revisited those darker days. Mahad was a whole year older than me and ran in a different pack than I did. He was the type of guy to only go to school to show off his new sneakers and insult other kids for wearing the knock offs. He was

82

a lot skinnier then and played basketball, making every friend of his a jock.

One day he attempted to cut me in line for lunch and shoved roughly past me. They were serving pizza in the cafeteria and I wanted to make sure I got there early in time to have some. I didn't want to be the kid who had to eat cold mozzarella sticks for lunch. When he pushed me that day I got angry and decided to stick up for myself. Mahad wasn't happy about that.

As one of the ruling czars of the school, no one had authority to speak back or question him.

So there in front of my friends and classmates he backhanded me. I threw a punch at his gut and must have landed it really well, because he was pissed. The next thing I knew he was jumping me with three of his other friends. The both of us were suspended for two days.

Ever since then, Mahad targeted me and made sure he got to see me suffer. He was in good with all the popular kids, and like the dictators they were, they ruled over everyone else. Some of my friends stopped speaking to me full-stop, and other kids would throw things at me any chance they got. One day, I heard I was going to get jumped after sixth period. I got really afraid and left for home that day early.

At community events, Mahad would point me out to his friends and they'd take turns shoving and punching me. One summer he created a rumor about me dating a boy. My parents found out about it, made me give up my phone and enforced a strict curfew. People believed I was gay for years. As a straight Muslim kid from a religious community, that didn't make my life any easier.

I unlocked my car and grabbed one of the plastic bags on the seat. I checked to see if it had all that I needed, and then locked the car when I got done. The only trace of the rain was in the puddles that were scattered around parts of the street. I dodged a big one and quickly crossed over to the house. At the mat I quickly wiped down my shoes again and made my way inside.

When I got back to the living room, *Abti* was grabbing a hold of Mahad's right shoulder as he recited *Quran*. Mahad had his head raised up at the ceiling as he swayed from side to side.

Abti turned to look at me. "That took you long enough. Quick, hand me one of the water bottles."

I dug through the plastic bag and pulled out a small bottle. I quickly handed it to him, and *Abti* took it from me.

He looked down at it confused. "I asked for the water. Where's your head today boy?"

"Sorry," I muttered under my breath, replacing the oil I'd given him for water.

I stood still as *Abti* recited every so often flicking water on Mahad's face. He didn't seem to be bothered by it and continued his swaying.

Had I felt bad for him? Of course. I would have never believed Mahad would have *sihr* put over him. He was loved and feared by all in our grade. *Feared.* I hadn't been the only kid he bullied.

Some other guys had it way worse than me. I once heard Mahad broke a freshman's jaw because he stepped on his brand new shoes. He was lethal and everyone was extremely afraid of what he could do to them. People lowered their heads when they walked past him. No one wanted any trouble from the king.

Abti continued reciting and throwing bits of water at Mahad. His body was there, but his mind wasn't. It was as if his brain had floated up to the ceiling, and he was waiting for it to fall back into place in his skull. Was this karma? Had *Allah* punished him for all the awful things he did to myself and others years ago? Or was this the doing of some other poor soul who had to endure his cruel insults and attacks?

"What's he just standing there for?" Aden asked Husni. *Abti* turned towards me.

I quickly got into action, and began taking out the rest of the waters and oils from the bag. Husni helped me set them near *Abti*. I pulled the *kitaab* open to the thirty sixth chapter and began reading in a low voice.

"Louder boy," *Abti* muttered between verses. I raised my voice at a steady pace, and glanced up at Mahad.

His eyes were meeting mine now. The pupils of his eyeballs were like two marbles floating in miniature fish bowls. He was like a cutout cardboard picture of his old self, no longer able to communicate or interact. He was the dummy in the ventriloquist's possession. It was a far cry from the Mahad I had grown to know over the years. His arrogance was long gone and replaced by an infant-like naivety that made the hairs on the back of my neck rise.

How was it that magic could do this to a person? And why would anyone want to inflict someone with something so awful in the first place? I could understand the pain if it were someone he bullied but it wasn't right going about revenge this way.

Who was to know if he'd ever get better? Nowadays the only magic people used was the darkest and most evil kind. It could be years before the spell was broken and he could be cured.

I could feel Husni looking at me while I stared blankly away at Mahad. I broke eye contact with him and began reading from the *musxaf* before me. Husni shuffled around and leaned towards his brother. I felt uncomfortable all of a sudden and tried distracting my mind from what they may have been saying. It had to have been about me and the strange way I was acting.

I looked up to see Aden glaring in my direction, as well as Husni's hawk-like gaze fixated on me.

Abti didn't seem to notice, and continued reciting verses and splashing water at Mahad.

"I think we can handle things from here on out." Husni said aloud, breaking *Abti's* focus as he stopped reciting. I looked at him, then Aden, and lastly *Abti*. What had he meant?

"I don't understand," *Abti* said, speaking my very thought aloud. Husni cleared his throat, and glanced at his brother.

"We just don't need any extra help is all. You're more than welcome to go home," he said, while looking straight at me.

Abti chuckled. "He's with me, always. Does he make you uncomfortable?"

Aden coughed. "*Yes*. Yes he does actually."

I frowned and then looked back to *Abti* who seemed to be every bit as confused as me.

"Well…I guess that would have to be up to him to decide. Would you like to leave Loyan?"

I froze. What was I expected to say in that moment? I turned my attention to Mahad, who was drooling from his mouth suddenly.

"Quick, go grab a towel. He wasn't doing that all day." Aden grumbled, as Husni went up to do as he was told.

Abti sighed. "It won't be an easy road for him from here on out."

Aden grunted. "Yes, I understand, but I have faith that *Allah* will heal him when He sees fit."

"You're right, brother. Loyan, we should let *Allah* take care of him. It's all in His hands after all."

"*Abti*, what do you mean?" I asked confused. Aden looked between the both of us.

Abti sighed, and turned to Aden. "If *Allah* wills it, then he shall get better. Keep your faith in Him. We're going to be heading home now. Help me up, boy."

I got up hesitantly. "*Abti*, what are you doing?"

Aden stood up as well, in a huff. "You have no right to leave now, old man. Stay put where you are and finish what you started."

Husni returned with a wad of paper towels for Mahad. "What's this? Where are they going?"

Abti took my hand as I helped him to his feet. Before he could, I bent down to grab his cane resting against the sofa. Aden got to it before I could. He held it back defensively.

"I'm not a rude or brash man, but this is completely ridiculous. You aren't going anywhere."

Abti sighed, and shook his head. "Insolent man." In the next moment he grabbed Aden by his shirt and twisted his arm and forced him to drop the cane he was clenching.

"*Abti*!" I cried out, stunned by what I just witnessed.

Abti said nothing more and walked towards the door. I followed him and fumbled with my shoes at the front. *Abti* slipped into his sandals, and we walked out of the house in seconds.

"Why did you do that *Abti*? Those people needed your help." I said trying to sound convincing.

Abti set his hand over my shoulder. "Yes they did, but not everyone is worth the effort. I didn't like the way those men spoke to you and me. They showed no respect. God be with that boy, but if he's got those two around, he won't have very much luck!"

Abti showed another side of himself I never seen before, in all my years of working alongside him. Something came over me and I had to tell him. *Abti* made his way to his jeep, and I stood in front of his car door before he could reach it.

"Out of the way boy! I'm not going back in there and you can't make me!"

"*Abti*, would you believe me if I told you that boy - Mahad used to bully me back in high school?"

He was silent, and then nodded. "No wonder you were acting so strange. Of course I can believe it."

I sighed. "I didn't know who to expect and then I saw it was him - *wallahi* I was so shocked."

Abti nodded and turned in the direction of the house. "And just look how *Allah* dealt with him for you. Our God doesn't like oppressors and transgressors."

"But it's not right, is it? For him to be that way - you can't say it was *Allah's* will."

"Listen to me: I can't speak for God, but I know that he would never allow a person to inflict any harm on someone as noble as you. You my boy are what Somalis call *'rag'*. Don't forget for a second that *Allah* wages war on anyone who hurts one of His friends. Now let me be. I need to sleep. Get home safe, and don't use your phone while driving. Goodnight."

I watched as *Abti* got into his car and drove off into the night. He'd never spoken so kindly to me as he had in that moment. I couldn't understand *Abti* for the life of me, but I loved him like a father.

Standing alone in the street, I looked towards the house we had just left, and considered *Abti's* words. *A friend of Allah's.* I never felt so unworthy of a compliment before.

Going back to my car, I realized I left some of the bottles and oils in the house. I didn't want to go back but something in me was itching to.

 I remembered how the men exchanged looks as they spoke about me. I had made them "uncomfortable." Was it worth going back inside and facing more trouble? I couldn't be sure, but I knew one thing: I wouldn't leave *Abti's* work undone.

Mahad needed my help, no matter how much pain he had inflicted on me. He was in need of assistance and so I would offer my services. It didn't matter to me that things had spoiled between his family and mine. If I were Mahad, I would have expected the same to be done for me. Besides, there was something about this job that demanded my very best.

Walking back to the house felt strange, but I welcomed the change. Knocking once, I stood outside their door again and waited. I wouldn't ring the bell no matter how much I wanted to.

I peered down at my shoes then and realized they didn't belong to me. I had mistakenly put on the wrong pair. I smiled, knowing I now had good reason to go back.

Allah made no mistakes, and this was no exception.

NASIIB

The studio was starting to feel a lot smaller than its nine hundred square feet. The crowdedness filled me with anxiety. With my return home tomorrow, I was feeling like one big hot mess. Laura undoubtedly sensed my unease about the trip.

"It's going to be a lot of stress. Family weddings always are, but you'll be coming back home to me! Think of *that* as your silver lining."

I laughed and pulled out a carton of orange juice from the fridge. Laura turned her attention away from the stovetop to me. She was making her famous skillet lasagna again.

"I told you about my family right? They're *My Big Fat Greek Wedding* times a hundred," Laura said, waving her wooden spoon into the air. Droplets of red sauce splattered across the ground.

"I thought you said you were Italian?" I asked, while pulling a cup out from the cabinet.

Laura chuckled. "I am."

I sighed, pouring myself a tall glass of orange juice.

"It's going to be so weird. Everyone will notice me. I haven't been back in years!"

Laura winked. "Hey, since when was that such a bad thing?"

"Oh my God Laura! I'm not trying to get married! I like where I'm at right now. Don't become one of those women on me." I laughed to no end at her silliness.

Laura brushed her hair behind her ears and held her right hand up in surrender. "I'm just saying. I love being your roommate and all but it'd be amazing to see you hitched. Can you imagine? I'd make *thee* greatest bridesmaid in the world," she exclaimed with glee.

"Well, you can keep waiting. That's not happening anytime soon. I'm there for one wedding and it is not going to be mine."

Laura sighed and shot me an amused look. "So what would they call women like us where you're from? Educated and working with zero-to-no chance of finding a guy."

"It's 'spinster' in any language," I replied without hesitation. Laura cracked up at that.

I set the glass in the sink and gave it a quick rinse. "I'm heading off to bed. I'll need a good night's sleep."

"Good night and good luck!" she called out.

"Thanks!" I shouted, heading into my bedroom. I shut the door behind me and trudged over to my mattress.

Just a few days ago I had been doing a lackluster job of presenting my colleagues with a new business module. After weeks of preparation and research I still managed to bomb it.

Fortunately for me, I had my roommate Laura to help me forget all about it over carne asada tacos and a reality TV marathon. The only plans I had for the weekend were to go hiking with my coworkers and do some shoe shopping at The Grove. Then Monday would predictably roll around and I'd be back at work. But fate would have it another way.

Three days ago I received a message from my younger cousin, Noora. She was getting married to a guy from her university's Muslim Students Association and invited me to be a part of her wedding on the fifth of this month. That was only two nights away. I had mixed feelings.

For one, I was over the moon for Noora. She was my baby cousin and one of the sweetest people I had ever known. I was overjoyed to hear of her news and anxious at the same time.

And yet it meant something much deeper for me: going home again.

I never came back since graduating from college. A large part of me didn't know what to expect with my return. I hadn't exactly left on good terms or with anyone's blessings. It was either going to go one of two ways: horribly and regrettably wrong or just bearably *okay*. I'd be smack dab in the middle of the seesaw, watching anxiously to see which way it would end for me.

****

The next morning Laura surprised me with a big beautiful breakfast before I took off. She had really gone all out. Most mornings, the both of us settled for burnt toast and coffee. On this particular occasion, she set the table with crispy turkey bacon, butter pancakes, scrambled eggs, and hash browns.

"You never told me you could make hash browns," I said, piling a generous helping of some onto my plate. They were cooked to crispy, golden brown perfection.

Laura shrugged, smiling. "What can I say? I'm a woman of many talents."

I added two pancakes onto my plate, along with a smaller helping of eggs, and turkey bacon. I'd never been too big of a fan of either but I didn't want Laura to get offended.

"It looks amazing. Thank you," I said as I reached for the syrup across the table.

"No problemo. I had to make our last day together special. So, tell me: what is it about your hometown you're the most worried about?" Laura asked, taking a seat at the square sized table crammed into our tiny kitchen.

I looked up with wide eyes and a mouth full of eggs and bacon.

"Where do I begin?"

Laura snorted. "Yikes, is it that bad? I remember my folks were dying to get me out of the house after high school. Now it's like they're just waiting by the phone to hear back from me. Crazy how that works huh?"

I shook my head. "Mine are the complete opposite. My aunt tried to force me to stay. It was always her way or the highway. I mean, I was always grateful for her help...raising me and all, but it was my choice."

Laura sighed. "Could you imagine if you moved across the country? I mean, we're only two hours away from San Diego. You can visit anytime."

I laughed, cutting into the fluffy pancakes.

"You have no idea," I said, smiling to myself. Laura leaned forward.

"Try me."

I set my fork and knife down, and took a sip of the water next to me. Laura looked at me expectantly. We'd been roommates for years but I never told her much about my family, or my past in general. I could tell she was just dying to hear *something*.

"My aunt has this daughter my age. She was practically my sister growing up. As soon as I announced my plans to move here, she goes berserk. Promises she'll never speak to me again if I leave. It's been five years and I never heard from her since."

Laura's mouth fell open as she mouthed a silent *wow*. "That bad? Well jeez. I bet it won't be any fun seeing her then?"

I picked up my fork and knife again. "You bet your butt it won't be."

For a moment my mind drifted back to Fowzi. *Eedo* had called me two years ago to tell me about her wedding. She had gotten married to her high school sweetheart, a tall handsome man named Elias who she always admired. One year later, I got another call from *Eedo*, announcing Fowzi's divorce. I was stunned and saddened by the news. Most of all, I was hurt by her silence.

In the time it took her to go from married to divorced, I hadn't heard a peep from her. It was like I no longer existed in her world. As much as her silence killed me inside, I still felt for her. At the time, I wished I could reach out to her and give her some comforting words. After all she was still family. Laura yawned. "When are you leaving again?"

"Wow. You want me out already? I sure am feeling the love," I said jokingly. Laura smiled and rested her head over her folded arms on the table.

"Oh c'mon, you're the love of my life. Hey, tell your Aunt about me. Let her know you're in good hands."

I giggled at first and then burst into loud laughter. Laura lifted her head up suddenly with a look of surprise. "What? What's so funny?"

I shook my head. "Nothing...I just..."

The laughing only grew louder and stronger from there. I couldn't contain myself. Laura joined in as well. "Oh tell me! C'mon!"

I grew serious for a moment. "Remember when you nearly burned the apartment down cooking rice...oh and those hard boiled eggs too."

Laura snorted. "Jeez! I forgot to turn off the range. I'm sorry!"

"That poor pot. Who would have ever thought its life would be cut so short." I muttered shaking my head with a smile.

Laura cracked up. "Oh my God!"

The both of us sat there cackling for what seemed like a lifetime. My nine o'clock alarm rang me back to reality. I stopped laughing and quickly turned it off. Laura's laughter died down too.

"So why are you leaving early if you don't even want to be back?"
Laura set her hand against her cheek, her face still red from laughing.

"I'm not being given a choice. I spoke to my Aunt and she says I must come today. I guess she has her reasons." I shrugged and pushed my plate away from me.

Laura smiled. "I think she misses you a lot more than she lets on."

"I don't really think so but it's only three days. I think I can survive them."

Laura sighed. "Aah! I'm going to miss you Ramla." She wore a deep set frown on her face. I held my hands out to her and squeezed them.

"Me too. I'm feeling homesick already."

****

Two and a half hours later, I was back in my hometown, sunny San Diego.

For a moment it didn't look much different than L.A. Palm trees lined the narrow streets, and people were dressed like it was still summer. Things instantly began to change once I made my way into the East. *East Daygo-ED*. There were many names for it, but I'd always know it as home. City Heights.

Long gone were the coffee shops of the East Village and in their place were liquor stores and smoke shops. Glass bottles and trash collected on the street sides and the palm trees here seemed less picturesque. This was the San Diego not shown on postcards or television. As a kid, the many faces of my city had always taken me by surprise. All that separated the worlds of the rich and poor was a single highway.

I turned into 52nd street and admired the infamous block of my childhood. There were all kinds of people here. It wasn't very long before I spotted my first Somali person. I was stopped at a red light, while she stood at a bus stop across from me. She was covered in a thick grey *jilbaab* that hung loosely over her small frame. She seemed to be focusing on something in the distance. I managed to catch her gaze and smiled. Her lips pulled apart in a beautiful smile. She held her hand up to me in greeting.

I waved back cheerfully and passed through the green light. Something about her face reminded me of my own mother. They shared a kindness in their eyes that was hard to forget. I felt grateful to have had that interaction, however small it seemed. I continued driving down the road and reached the string of *halal* meat shops and *hawalads*. Little Mogadishu.

There were old men in *kufis* and baggy suit coats standing outside of halal butcher shops, clutching their canes and laughing out loud. Groups of women in *jilbaab* strolled along the sidewalks, and young men in crisp white *thobes* were headed towards the *masjid*. I'd forgotten it was Friday. They'd all be rushing to catch the Friday prayer.

While my car remained stopped at another red light, I watched as two middle aged Somali men illegally crossed the road. I watched with a deep anxiety and fear, reminded of my own *Aabo*. He'd been crossing this very same road when he was struck by an oncoming van. His fragile body was rushed to the ICU only for him to pass away a day later from injuries. It hurt to remember.

It hadn't even been a year later when *Hooyo* joined him. What seemed like an innocent lump in her left breast became the cause of her quick progression into illness. Having them out of my life at the age of seven burned a hole right through me. Orphaned and alone, Fowzi's mother swept me up, taking me in as her own. Growing up in their warm home full of love still left me aching for my dead parents. I suppose that was another reason for my hesitance to come back home. Every memory would come rushing back to me, good or bad. I knew I wouldn't be ready for any of them.

The person behind me began blaring their horn, so I switched my focus back onto the road. I glanced at my tank and realized I would need to fill up soon. Once I got the chance, I pulled into the nearest gas station and got out of my car. I could use some kind of a cold drink to relax my nerves.

****

Eedo hated my hair.

From the very moment I stepped inside her home, she was glaring at me in disapproval. A part of me expected she wouldn't be a fan. Chopping your hair off as a woman was one of the biggest offences in Somali culture. And yet living in LA all this time gave me a strong sense of confidence in my pixie haircut. Laura had even helped me add auburn streaks once I got it styled. I thought it was cute.

Without any hesitation *Eedo* unleashed her immediate disapproval for my new 'do.

"You look like a boy!" She twisted her lips into a frown. I stepped back, realizing there would be no friendly reunion between us. Only judgment.

I forced a smile. "*Eedo* I *like* the length. It's really easy to take care of. I only-"

"It's not the least bit attractive, especially at your age," *Eedo* narrowed her eyes at my hair. To think people back home adored my cut!

I sighed. "Well, I happen to like it, *Eedo*."

"You'll never find a man to marry you with hair shorter than his," she spat with fiery eyes.

That comment stung me the most.

"*Eedo* is having a man all that really matters in the world?" I said it with passion but I hadn't meant it. I was twenty seven and still unmarried. My hope of finding Mr. Right was beginning to look a little bleak.

All morning it was one comment after another from *Eedo*. My nose piercing was too edgy and would give me an infection. The white henna I had on my right hand was *ciyaal suuq* and couldn't hold a candle to traditional black henna. I had lost all my beautiful curves and would never attract a man with the body of a young boy. It was a suffocating environment to be around, but it was the only place I could go. Spending my time in a hotel room would be the utmost disrespect to *Eedo* and cause every woman to gossip. So I kept my silence and let her make all the comments she wanted to.

A while later *Eedo* backed down. I suppose she had her fill of commentary for the day. "Well, it's your life you're throwing away. Just go ahead and get changed already. There should be a *baati* on your bed."

Hearing those words gave me a feeling of deep peace. I hadn't worn a *baati* in years. There was something about the traditional loose cotton dress that made my heart grow soft. As soon as I slipped the *baati* over my head, something felt different.

Not only did it drape my frame in a loose, soft cotton, but it filled my heart with nostalgia; memories flashed before my eyes. I was taken back to days when *Eedo* would be wearing a bright *baati* while cooking, cleaning, and running errands on school nights. Her *baatis* always smelled of sweet detergent and were never wrinkly. She used to wear a long loose *jilbaab* over them while going out and about. Something in my heart sank remembering back to those days. I pictured Fowzi and me coming home from school to *Eedo*. We'd enter a house that smelled of sweet tea and *malaawax*. It was *Eedo's* afternoon specialty, and it made us love her all the more.

I smoothed out the burnt orange *baati* with my fingertips as I sat at the edge of my bed.

Noora mentioned she'd be away in LA up until the night of her wedding. She and a group of friends rented out a place in Baldwin Hills to celebrate her last few days of singledom. I knew Fowzi was still in the city, but wasn't sure where she was living. So that just left *Eedo* and me.

Fate could be a funny thing. I would have never thought the two of us would be living under the same roof again. It felt strange not having Noora or Fowzi around. The three of us would always back each other up against *Eedo's* scoldings. I'd have to grow some tougher skin if I was going to last three whole days here. *Eedo* wasn't going to change her nature all on account of me.

I stood up and looked around my old room. Fowzi and I had shared sixteen years here. I could just see her now, rushing into the room after school and heading straight to the radio. She'd blast a new jam from *B-95.5* and sing along to whatever was playing, word for word. Some days I'd be on my bed with homework sprawled all around me, begging her to shut it off.

"C'mon! It's too loud! Turn it down, at least!" I'd beg of her as she swayed around the room beautifully. Despite my pleading I'll admit that I loved watching her dance.

She'd swing her body from one edge of the room to the other, completely carefree. It was amazing. After a few minutes passed with me watching from across the room, she'd cross over with a smile and extend her hand and drag me up to my feet. We celebrated the rhythms of the music and bent our bodies in accordance to the tunes. Aside from the absence of the music and my homework scattered across the surface of my bed, not much had changed. Except for the air. It never felt so cold in here before.

Fowzi would've hated it.

****

Early the next morning, I woke up to the *adhaan* playing in the distance. The room was all darkness aside from the alarm clock in the corner. In bright red numbers the time read five twenty-six. I rubbed at my eyes and sat up in bed. I looked around the room, trying to place the various foreign objects all around me. It was only when I saw my suitcase in the corner that I remembered where I was.

A strange feeling washed over me again, especially as I got up out of bed. I tiptoed out of my room to the bathroom just across from my bedroom. I flicked on the light switch and turned the spout towards the blue. I always liked my water cold. While splashing the water over my face, I stopped to look at myself. I had been born and raised a Muslim.

All my life I'd been told not to eat pork, sing Christmas songs, or talk to boys. Most importantly, I was ordered to pray all five prayers on time each day. And yet it had been years since I'd consistently done that. The last time I remembered praying them was in college. But even then, it had gotten too hard to keep up with both studies and prayers. When the deadlines grew too close, I left my prayers to hover over my textbooks late into the night. This present moment had begun to feel artificial to me.

It dawned on me that there was no fooling God. He was the *All Seeing* and *All Hearing*.

He'd known how bad I'd been about completing my prayers. I hadn't worn *hijab* since my college years either. I had zero physical or spiritual attachment to my religion. I was just Muslim by name. Yet here I was at the crack of dawn, rinsing my face with cold water. I wanted to shut off the lights and crawl back into bed. A part of me had really wanted to, but another part continued rinsing my skin anyway. I stopped at my feet and then shut the water off. I grabbed a burgundy *jilbaab* that was folded in the closet and wrapped its warmth around me. I stood still for a minute and went over what I needed to say. It had been so long and I wanted to make sure I was saying it all right.

Once I felt it was time I began my prayer, "*Allahu Akbar.*"

The words fell loosely off my tongue. I tried to scrape them closer together.

Arabic hadn't been the only language I'd forgotten. I stood reciting *Surah Fatiha* in a low whisper.

"You alone do we worship, and You alone do we ask for help. Guide us on the straight path." After reading another *surah* I bent down halfway, stood back up, and then fell onto my hands and knees. My forehead was pressed against the rough carpet floor, with eyes wide open. Back at *dugsi*, they said this was the closest you could ever be to God in this life.

I recited more words in Arabic, and prayed silently for something more.

Eedo's health, the safety of her home, her peace of mind, and the happiness of Fowzi. *Ameen.*

****

The following day, I spent most of my afternoon in the living room. I had my work keeping my attention, with folders filled with things to look over. Eedo was napping on the sofa with her thick emerald green and gold *garbasaar* drawn over her.

I looked out the window and thought back to my younger years. In another time I'd be here in this very same spot looking out at the neighbors and cars going past. My eyes were itching, darting from corner to corner. I asked myself what happened to the boy with the blind father, or the girl with the three-legged dog. Why didn't the ice cream truck come down the street anymore with the sweet familiar tune that filled my childhood?

My thoughts led me back to Fowzi. Why hadn't I seen her yet? Where was she living these days? I wondered if my questions would be answered when I saw her at the wedding. She'd have to be there on her little sister's big day, *right?*

My questions were interrupted by *Eedo's* coughing. These days she kept a medicine for every ache and pain in her body. It was only years ago when she was raising three rowdy girls on her own. The only break she ever got was when we went to school and fell asleep. Splitting her time between working daycare and us, there was never any real rest. It was inevitable she would grow tired and weak, but this was my *Eedo*. The only real superhero of my youth. I struggled to accept her fragility.

Her bottom half was left uncovered as the window sent in a cool breeze. I got up then to pull her *garbasaar* over her body. I moved away from her quietly and went into the kitchen. Dinner was yet to be made. I'd take a much needed break from my work files and cook. I'd been in the kitchen lots recently. Laura taught me tons of Italian recipes and I had mastered most, if not all of them. When it came down to Somali food though I was a little rusty. I hadn't cooked it in all the years I'd been away from home. It had been ages since I last whipped up *baasto*, or *bariis*. I'd never been a big fan of either and always opted for cooking a chicken lasagna or stew.

I could imagine *Eedo* wouldn't be a very big fan of me diverting from the usual dinner options. Besides, she had always refused to eat anything with cheese, fearing it would affect her cholesterol levels. So *baasto* it was.

I opened the freezer to find there was a small bag of beef cubes tucked into the back. I pulled that out and had a look inside the fridge. There was half a red onion, some tomatoes, and a single green bell pepper. I bent over and grabbed each one. All of a sudden *Eedo* called out to me. I shot up instantly and banged my head against the bottom of the freezer door.

"Ow," I muttered while running my hand over my throbbing head. I stepped back and gently rubbed the area I hit. The pain felt so intense it made me stumble back in a daze.

"Ramla! *Nayaa* Ramla!" she exclaimed. I sighed and shut the fridge, going out into the living room.

"*Haa Eedo?*" I asked as she sat up, folding the *garbasaar* I'd just placed over her.

"I couldn't sleep with all the noise you were making. What are you up to back there?"

I smiled proudly. "I'm making *baasto*."

She sighed. "What is it with you and Noora? The fridge is already full of leftovers."

I didn't respond but watched as she ran her hands over her legs. "You can do whatever you like. Just go and get me my henna. It's on the counter in a bowl."

I walked off into the kitchen and looked around for the bowl in mention. There was one at the left side counter, farthest to the right. I lifted the aluminum covering to see it halfway filled with homemade henna. It was damp and murky brown, resembling mud after rainfall. I set the covering back on and carried it back into the living room. *Eedo* was looking out the window when I got back.

"Here's the henna, *Eedo*," I said, handing it to her. She broke her attention from the window and took it from my hands.

"While you're still around, you might as well open that letter for me over there. I forgot to check it before and it's been sitting there since last week." *Eedo* dabbed her fingers into the grey metal bowl.

I went over to the table nearest to the front door and picked up a single white envelope next to *Eedo's* keys. It was from her medical group. I opened it to read there was some information about an upcoming appointment. A minute more of reading and I discovered that *Eedo* had rheumatoid arthritis. At the very bottom of the letter was contact information for her clinic and insurance company. I was at a loss for words. An overwhelming feeling of emptiness ate away at my being. I glanced up at *Eedo* in disbelief. How could this be and why had I never been told of this? *Arthritis.*

She sighed. "Well, what does it say?"

I cleared my throat and folded the letter, placing it back into the envelope. I wouldn't mention my discovery to her.

"They're reminding you of an appointment this coming Tuesday. It's at one thirty. Do you already know?" My voice was shaking. I couldn't stop myself from looking at her hands. They were whole and moving, decorated in wet henna. Nothing seemed weak about them.

She nodded. "Yes. I have it written down somewhere."

I watched her as she silently painted the rest of her fingertips on her left hand. She hummed quietly as she dipped them back into the bowl. All these years I'd been away and I never thought to ask about her health. My eyes began to cloud, *Eedo's* image blurring in front of me. A single tear escaped and ran down my cheek. I turned away from her and hurried into the kitchen. Another tear came crashing down into my open palms.

I sobbed silently and thought of the pain that filled *Eedo's* joints. The pins and needles that disrupted her peace. I would have never found out had it not been for that letter. *Eedo* was never one to reveal anything and I'd always been too self absorbed to ask. I thought of going back into the living room and talking to her about it but felt too

106

ashamed. What good would my sudden concern for her do? I felt dirty from the guilt. Selfish and low. *Eedo* was silently suffering, and my pity would never change that.

****

That night after cooking, I put some incense on the burner and set it on the floor in the center of the living room. It wasn't long before the sweet aroma of the *uunsi* wafted through the air around me. *Eedo* had gone out to do some last minute wedding shopping, so I'd have a quiet night to myself. She found it strange that I wanted to be cooped inside all day. But I hadn't minded at all. She assumed I was trying to hide away from old friends.

All of the friends I once had in the city were distant acquaintances to me now. Besides, I didn't want anyone to feel obliged to host me or take me out. I'd see everyone I was meant to see tomorrow night at the wedding. Anything before that was unnecessary. There were too many memories in San Diego for my liking. Going out would only reveal each and every one to me. I could do without the hurt. I reached for a *garbasaar* from the chair and wrapped it around myself.

There was something I needed to see before I left.

I turned on the flashlight on my phone and dug through one of the drawers in the old china cabinet. I shifted through the heap of bad report cards Fowzi and I tucked away over the years. It had to be under them somewhere. I looked for a few seconds more before pulling it out. *Aha!* The family album.

Back in high school Fowzi and I pulled some money together to buy one ourselves. We hated that all our family pictures had been scattered around the house and unorganized. So after school one day, we purchased an album for fifteen whole bucks at *Rite Aid*. Every picture of the family's was stored in there. I ran my hands over the smooth surface. It had grown a little worn around the edges, but for the most

107

part the green velvet hadn't lost its beauty. Nor had the words, "family" and "love" etched in gold cursive across the cover.

I made my way to the sofa and flipped through the delicate pages of the album. The first photograph I saw was at the zoo. Fowzi and I had gone there for a school field trip in the fifth grade. We were flashing wide, excited smiles and draping our skinny arms around each other. Everything from our tops to our cross bodies had been matching. Fowzi's black *hijab* was drawn loosely over her head, revealing some curly strands of hair. My *hijab* was wrapped tightly around my head. It had always been that way up until recent years.

I continued flipping through the pages till I got to one of *Eedo* and Fowzi. It was at *Colina Park* during *Eid*. They had both been dressed in aqua blue and black. I'd taken that picture. I hadn't remembered *Eedo* smiling as brightly as she did then.

There was another of *Eedo* and her ex husband, Dahir. It was back in Kenya. They were standing side by side in *Dadaab* refugee camp. Dahir had his arms crossed tightly together while *Eedo* looked to be leaning into him. Neither was smiling. I saw another of Fowzi, Noora, and I. We were in the backyard, lying in the grass. There was a cat that had been wandering into people's backyards that day. We spent most of our time expecting to find it but never did. In the picture Noora was sitting in front of me, and Fowzi was holding an orange water gun and sticking her tongue out behind us. I tried to remember why I seemed to be laughing so hard.

I came across another of *Eedo*. It was during *Ramadan* and she just finished praying. Fowzi made her take the picture as I stood in the background sticking up the peace sign. *Eedo* looked a little tired and ill there. I was nearly halfway through the album when I realized something I'd been trying to ignore for too long. I missed Fowzi.

Over the past five years, it had been hard not hearing from her. It was like there'd been a deep hole drilled into me because of it. I wanted her to be in my life again. She was my best friend and sister. As a kid I wouldn't have dreamed of us growing apart. Now the ugly reality of our distance was beginning to disturb me. I shut the album and set it gently to my side. I promised myself right then that I wouldn't go back home without seeing her. I didn't care if she didn't want to speak to me. I needed to see her.

I missed everything about Fowzi- from her beautiful smile to her crazy laughter. But I knew better than to expect any of it. All these years apart had created a divide between us. The wedding of someone we both loved wasn't going to change that.

****

The wedding hall was still nearly empty at nine pm. I should have known better. It was a Somali wedding after all. Everyone was going to turn up hours later than they were supposed to. Maybe I was a bit naive to think that was going to change tonight.

Eedo had been in such a rush before, but now she was roaming idly around the dance floor, looking for something to do. It must have been an exciting and nerve-wrecking night for her. Her baby all grown up and soon to be someone's wife. She never wore her emotions on her sleeve, but I could tell there were some feelings cooking inside her.

I stood up to adjust my baggy *dirac* once more. I was fairly tall at 5'11, but felt as if I was still drowning in my *dirac*. Aside from that, I was a bit self conscious. *Eedo's* comments about my curve less body were still circulating in my mind. She was right, of course. After all the diets and cardio the weight of my younger years was long gone.

I was sitting alone at my table, so that could be adding to the insecurity too. Most girls wouldn't dare coming to an *aroos* solo. Especially if the bride or groom was family or a close friend. I must have looked a bit strange. Maybe that was why two women at the table across from me kept staring at me. *Did they know me?* Neither of their faces looked very familiar to me.

Smiling, I realized it was common for my Somali people to stare a hole through one another at first sight. I turned my attention to my phone on the table to check my makeup. I pursed my lips slightly to check if there was any red lipstick on my teeth. Nothing. My highlight was looking okay too. I glanced back up at the two girls.

They looked like they could have been sisters. The one with the bob styled hair and hoop earrings smiled. I did too, and in the next moment she stood up and was coming towards me. Her friend or sister stayed put, still keeping a curious eye on me. I cleared my throat nervously as she approached.

"Hey *abaayo*. Aren't you related to Noora?" She flashed a bright white smile, and seemed nice enough.

"Yes. I'm Ramla, we're first cousins," I answered pulling my lips apart in a small smile. The other girl's attention perked once I spoke. She wasn't hiding the fact that she was watching me at all.

"*Ma sha Allah.* I had a feeling you were. My name's Bahja. You probably don't remember me, do you?" She extended her hand out to me.

I sat forward to shake her hand, looking at her closely. She didn't look very familiar to me. Maybe she was one of Fowzi's old friends.

"Sorry, I don't. Can you refresh my memory? I'm sorry, *abaayo*," I said, setting my purse in my lap. I clenched it tightly, feeling more anxious by the minute. She sat down on the chair next to mine and laughed.

"Crawford. We took history and physical ed. together. That's my sister over there, Rahma. She's Noora's age."

I nodded, meeting her younger sister's eyes and turned back to her now.

Bahja was looking me up and down like she was checking for something. She flashed another friendly smile. "So, are you still living in SD?"

I shook my head. "No. I moved after college. I'm over in LA right now."

"Ooh, that's dope. What's it like over there?" she asked, leaning forward with excitement.

I smiled. "Not much different than here really. Have you been there before?"

She sighed. "Of course, but only to visit. I want to try moving out there sometime. I can't stand it here. Everyone in each other's business. *Wallahi* I'm so over it."

I nodded. "I know what you mean."

"Are there any cute guys there?" she asked with a smirk. The questions were piling up now.

I laughed. "There's some, but I'm too focused on my work to notice."

"Oh okay. So what do you do for a living?" She rested her head against her hand listening. I felt like I was in the hot seat of an exclusive interview. This girl was making it seem like I was the most interesting person in the world.

"I'm in marketing. It's really boring," I replied, remembering all the countless work files I left at *Eedo's* place. They would need my attention soon.

"Ugh, I wish I could go out there. I don't want to live with my mom till I get married. I need to see the world and be my own person, you know? You're so lucky to be living alone. I envy you."

"I don't actually live alone. I have a roommate," I said all of a sudden. She looked a little less impressed hearing that.

"Oh. Well, that's realistic. Rent aint cheap."

I smiled and turned to her sister who was narrowing her eyes at me now.

Bahja laughed hysterically. "Sorry if I'm being so annoying. Anyway, have you seen Fowzi yet?"

I listened more closely now. "No, why do you ask?"

"Just curious. She's your cousin, right? Did you happen to hear about the divorce? It's so sad *wallahi*."

"Yeah," I muttered crossing and uncrossing my leg.

"She didn't deserve that - she's such a *miskiin*. Men are such pigs *wallahi*," she grumbled frowning.

"What? I'm not following," I said, scooting my chair a bit closer now.

Bahja furrowed her eyebrows. "You mean you don't know?"

I shook my head. "No. Can you tell me?"

She sighed. "Elias cheated on her. The entire time they were married he was talking to another chick. Poor girl didn't know until some heifer in Minneapolis started telling everyone that she was engaged to her man!"

"What?" I asked in disbelief. That couldn't be.

Bahja nodded. "He was trying to marry her low-key without Fowzi knowing. Such a dog, *wallahi*."

"Wow," I muttered in complete shock. *Eedo* had never mentioned that to me over the phone. I felt a hot sting in my chest, and all I wanted to do was get up and leave.

"She did right by dumping him. Cheaters will never be faithful and pretty boys will always be players."

I sat in silence trying to make sense of it all. Meanwhile Bahja was going on and on about Elias- his cheating and other unsavory habits. Suddenly she stopped speaking, noticing how quiet I'd been after all this time.

She reached out to touch my hand. "No one ever told you any of this, huh?"

I shook my head. She made an 'O' shape with her mouth, and turned back around to her sister. I could feel her staring at me as I sat there, unable to speak. Silence iced the air as I sat there at a complete loss for words.

"Ramla."

I looked up to see none other than Fowzi before me. She wore a satin burgundy shawl over her curly jet black hair. Her wide brown eyes bore into me as she managed a small smile.

"Hey girl! How are you?!" Bahja exclaimed before pulling her into a tight hug. I met Fowzi's eyes as she drew one arm around the girl's back. Bahja's sister Rahma was getting up all of a sudden.

"I was just asking about you. It's been so long!" Bahja said. Fowzi smiled, and stepped back. Rahma was next as she gave her a squeeze as well.

I looked downward, feeling relief wash over me. The anxiety wasn't so much as an afterthought now. I took the time to look at Fowzi, while she shared some words with the sisters. Her face looked slimmer now but the rest of her hadn't changed much at all. She still resembled the wide eyed, goofy girl I shared so many years of my youth with. Tall, beautiful, and radiant Fowzi.

A moment later she was walking back to the table towards me. This time alone. Bahja and Rahma were quickly trekking off in the opposite direction, past the table they'd been sitting at minutes earlier.

Fowzi pulled a chair out next to me. "How's it going?"

"*Alhamdulilah*, I can't complain. How have you been?" I asked her, clearing my throat.

She shrugged. "I'm doing alright."

Her response was accompanied with a short bout of silence from the both of us. I tried to force away the gulp in my throat but it wasn't easy. It had been years.

"How's life in the city of angels?" she asked, breaking the silence.

"It's been good. I feel like a local now," I replied grinning.

Fowzi smiled. "I'm happy for you. Is work good?"

"Yeah, it's great," I said, smoothing my hands nervously over my dress. She turned back around to the empty dance floor and laughed. I froze hearing it. So many memories of her surged into my mind in a matter of seconds.

"Noora's wedding already. Life goes by fast."

"I know right? It's crazy," I said, looking down.

More silence. Fowzi looked to me as her eyes grew a bit damp, "I'm sorry things got so ugly between us."

I didn't speak, and waited for her to go on for an explanation. Fowzi sighed. "I was afraid to be alone. I thought we'd do it all together. Finding jobs after college and going to each other's weddings."

"I was scared too, Fowzi. I didn't think I could do it all on my own. Nobody makes it out in LA."

Fowzi glanced up at me. "But you did. Now look at you. You made us all proud."

I didn't know how to respond to that. Did she mean Eedo too? As far as I knew nothing about me seemed to bring her any pride.

"I wanted to tell you about the wedding - I did. I was just so overwhelmed with everything. Then the divorce happened. It broke me, Ramla."

"I'm sorry," I muttered, tears piercing my eyes. Something in her face changed and I wanted to reach out and hug her.

Fowzi leaned forward. "I loved him and he cheated. I gave him all of me and that was never enough."

"He didn't deserve you," I said with a shaky voice.

Fowzi laughed. "*Calaf* - it was written. *Bas*, what more can I say or do?"

I groaned and looked up at her. "I never liked him."

Fowzi was quiet and then erupted with laughter. She grabbed a hold of my knees as she chuckled hard.

"*Xaasidat*, you're telling me this now? Oh my God!"

"*Wallahi*, I didn't! He was always getting seconds at lunch and kissing up to every teacher. Ugh, I hated him."

Fowzi giggled like the carefree twenty two year old I last remembered her as.

I smiled. "*In sha Allah* you'll find better. I know you will. Just look at you."

Fowzi wiped at her eyes and gave me a look. "Oh please. I look so much older now but you don't look a day over eighteen. I think you might be a vampire."

"Yeah right! I had to start using anti aging cream," I confessed, much to her surprise.

Fowzi's eyes grew wide. "Say *wallahi?*"

"I swear! I went to the drugstore the other day. I got two. One for me and my roommate," I said.

"Me too!" Fowzi exclaimed laughing even harder.

"Oh my God!" I joined in almost tearing up with all the giggling.

Fowzi sighed. "So, how long are you here for?"

"I got work tomorrow, so just tonight."

"Aah, that sucks. Back to reality, eh? Well, if you ever come back down again, give me a call."

"I will, for sure," I said, smiling brightly.

"I'm happy for you," she said. "You got everything you ever wanted."

I sat up a little. "Did I?"

"Yeah. Great job, your own life. And don't ever try feeling bad about it either," Fowzi said resting her hand on my knee.

"I'm really glad I got to see you. We needed this," I admitted, feeling at peace.

Fowzi nodded. "You know I always asked God to forgive me. For cutting you off all these years. I just-"

She covered her hands over her eyes suddenly and began crying. I looked around the room and then reached out to touch her shoulder. She didn't let up.

"Hey..." I whispered. "We're good now. I promise."

Fowzi raised her head and wiped at her eyes. Her mascara barely saved by seconds.

"He married her three weeks ago. Happily ever after huh?" Fowzi muttered, as a single tear fell down her face.

"Fowzi - c'mon you don't need him. Forget that loser!"

She laughed. "Oh God-I'm going to ruin my makeup."

"Wanna go to the bathroom?" I asked. "Before all the *habos* start piling in."

Fowzi smiled. "Yeah."

I got up and waited for her to follow suit. She sniffled and turned back around. The two sisters from before were staring at us. The next second they peeled their eyes away and peered down at their phones.

"I hate those two. I always have," Fowzi said, laughing. I smiled and pulled my arm around her.

"It's going to be alright, Fowzi. Everything works out for the better. Just trust in His plan," I said.

Fowzi nodded. "You were always the smart one."

I smiled. "And you were always the beautiful one."

Fowzi laughed. "*Nasiib kayga.*"

I playfully shoved her. "C'mon, I think I have some mascara in my bag."

Fowzi followed me towards the bathroom. In that moment, something was different.

I tried putting a finger on it. Maybe the air was less thick. Or maybe we didn't care so much about what the sisters thought of us. I suppose my dress wasn't dragging against the floor anymore. It could have very well been Fowzi. She always had a way of bringing out the best in me.

I couldn't be sure of the exact feeling but happiness sure came close.

Hooyo Macaan

Qalanjo. Caadey. Quruxley.

She had sandy brown skin with a likeness of gold in the sunlight. *Tima Hindi* that swept past her small rounded shoulders. Dazzling and bright *indho deeraleey* perched over her slim nose. Plump lips that were often pulled apart to display a wide *fanax* and striking *cirad madoow*. *Dhax dhuuban* that drove men wild and women even wilder with envy. A stunning woman in all respects of the word.

My *Hooyo*: the most beautiful woman in her village. Holding the admiration of everyone that beheld her and yet her beauty could only be matched with much more. As the eldest daughter of a poor farmer and midwife, she was no stranger to hard work. It was the very foundation her family lived upon. She'd till the land, milk the cows, feed the livestock and walk six miles to the city and back carrying the goods her father harvested. Her determination and strength were unmatchable. She worked with the fierceness of the summer heat that would send its rays mercilessly down upon her. Working just as hard as any man, if not more.

Despite all that she did for her family, life would soon cast an undeniable reminder upon her. She was a young woman in the Somali countryside and like any young woman she needed to be married. "It was only a matter of time," *Hooyo* would later tell me.

According to her parents she was getting too old at just nineteen. Girls her age and younger were already on their second or third pregnancy. They didn't want to deny her a similar chance at life. All of *Hooyo's* efforts for the family were appreciated but marriage was the best route she could take. It was a rite of passage that would ensure the family's

119

honor, respect and wealth for years to come. Soon *Hooyo* left the fields as the doors of courtship were opened to her.

It wasn't long before a rich man from *Xamar* came and paid a brief visit to *Hooyo's Aabo*. He, like many others, heard talk of an astonishingly beautiful woman that worked harder than any man in her village. Unlike many others, he was wealthy and came from a well-known family. *Awoowe* gave him his blessings and requested a hefty *yarad* of one hundred cows and fifty-five goats.

In no longer than two weeks, *Hooyo* married the man who would later become my father. Grandfather was given what he asked for and all was good and well. After the *aroos Hooyo* moved to the city with my *Aabo*. Soon her stomach grew big with a baby boy. Nine months later my oldest brother, Mohamed was born. Everyone delighted at the news and sent their congratulations to my parents.

Hooyo would give *Aabo* three more sons before they fled to America in the year of 1993. The family of six soon relocated to sunny San Diego and seven months later I was born. From what I'm told I was a difficult baby and cried endlessly during the late hours of the night. *Hooyo* grew sick shortly after my birth and was hospitalized for three weeks and four days.

Things only grew from bad to worse after that. My father's *Hooyo* back in *Xamar* was dying and bedridden. Her illness was unknown to doctors and family, so it was presumed she was dying of old age. Upon hearing the news *Aabo* went straight to the airport to book an emergency flight to be with her. She died three hours before he landed. *Aabo* loved his mother more than anything. He was left devastated by her passing.

Aabo flew back to America weeks later and was never the same since. In time he left his taxi job and grew accustomed to living a life that granted him endless leisure. It wasn't very long until my once hard-working *Aabo* filed for welfare and began receiving food stamps. He turned in his honor for a handout and would come back home at odd hours of the night. His time and undivided attention was given to other Somali men at the coffee shop on 52nd street. Without fail, he took his place there every morning with the other *fadhi ku dirir* as his company.

Meanwhile, *Hooyo* settled into the typical Somali housewife role. She devoted all of her time and energy into it. A day didn't go by where she didn't cook the family breakfast, lunch and dinner. *Shaah* was made fresh each day at four p.m, like clockwork. *Uunsi* engulfed the house, every nook and cranny smelled of the strong burning incense. This was her routine. *Hooyo* would only sleep peacefully when she finished cleaning the house from top to bottom each night. No dish was ever left dirty.

Outside of everyday chores and cooking, *Hooyo's* week didn't consist of very much. Unable to speak or understand English, she couldn't sit back on the sofa to unwind and watch television like any other housewife in America would. Sometimes I'd find her at the couch after a long day of work wearing a lost look over her face. It was like she was asking herself what brought her to this place in life.

All the time *Hooyo* spent sitting and stressing contributed to her rapid weight gain. My mother's fabled waist was no longer in sight. The last she seen a doctor she weighed in at a shocking 285lbs. Despite a demand for intense exercise and activity from doctors, *Hooyo* remained inactive. She'd spend her silent hours applying henna on her hands as she listened to the booming voices of men on *BBC Radio Somalia.*

Hooyo couldn't find comfort in confiding in her family either. Relatives and friends back in Somalia would call her often but only to pass their quick greetings followed by requests. They'd give her their artificial hellos and would soon get to the real reason behind their calls. Like any other Somali, *Hooyo's* family expected her to send them large amounts of money to support them. In their minds they still believed

121

Hooyo to be the strong, hard working woman she once been in her youth.

They undoubtedly pictured her carrying her old strengths to the new land and perhaps holding a job or two. Little did they know she was never employed and had been a monthly recipient of food stamps and cash assistance. They must have perceived *Aabo* to still be the wealthy man he once been as well. *Hooyo* realized this and would refrain from speaking to her family as much as possible.

She once shared a close relationship with my oldest brother, Mohamed. That was until he got married. As a kid I used to watch him sip tea in the afternoon with *Hooyo* as they listened to *BBC* radio together. Hours would trickle away like minutes as they discussed Somali politics. Now all his time and conversations were dedicated to his wife of three years, Nimo. He hardly ever called or even visited *Hooyo*, or any of us for that matter. I could only imagine how much it killed *Hooyo* inside.

My two other brothers Faisal and Kamal were always working and never had time to spare for *Hooyo* either. Aden, my fourth oldest brother was the *ciyaal suuq* of the family. So his relationship with *Hooyo* was a bit muddled as it was. The only conversation he shared with her was the frequent scolding and lecture he was recipient of for staying out so late. *Aabo* was never really home. He would spend his days with other men, who like him refused to forget the past and move forward with their lives. Then there was me, *Hooyo's* only daughter. The one child you'd expect to have an undying relationship with her mother.

With assurance I could say I always been an obedient daughter to *Hooyo*. I would do all that she asked of me and more. Unfortunately, that's as much as I could say. Neither of us would ask each other how we were doing or what we'd been up to. We didn't speak as much as a mother and daughter should have.

On her weekends, *Hooyo* would invite woman who she'd call friends over for tea and treats. These so called friends of hers were the kind that didn't shy away from gossip and idle talk. I remember always telling myself these same women would speak badly about *Hooyo* one day too. These women left no stone unturned in their talks. Everyone in the Somali community seemed to be an open topic of discussion for them, including myself.

Whenever I was with *Hooyo* they would be quick to flash their bright smiles, unending greetings, and proclaim how good of a daughter I was. Yet when they'd catch me alone I was an easy target for them. They'd make nothing but snide remarks about me. Like how I looked nothing like my mother and didn't share her beautiful light complexion. Or why I hadn't graduated or married yet like their daughters had. When cornered like this I'd always have to smile or laugh their comments away. *Hooyo* had taught me to always respect my elders, even if they weren't deserving of an ounce of it.

I would like to think these tea times were the sole cause of *Hooyo's* diabetes onset. There was never a shortage of *xalwad, buskud* or *dolsho* at any of these gatherings. *Hooyo* would always make sure to have us kids restock treats days ahead. I could just picture *Hooyo* passing the time, chatting away and placing one greasy and sugar filled lump of *xalwo* after another into her mouth. She'd lose track of how many times she indulged in the sweets while allowing herself one more. I imagined she believed she deserved a sweet reward for all the work she'd done during the week. "*Treat yourself*", *Hooyo* might say. "*It can't hurt.*"

My once unbreakable *Hooyo* had fell victim to *sonkor,* or the sugar disease as Somalis called it. Type II diabetes was the diagnosis. She became another Somali parent who failed to distinguish the thin line between comfort and food. Sometimes I couldn't help but look at my mother and cry. It was beyond depressing to think she left a *life* in her motherland. A life that gave her admiration and strength for a foreign land in which she drew blood from her fingertip daily.

123

I remember the day I found *Hooyo* crying. It started out like any other. I was upstairs working on a homework assignment while watching the latest episode of *Sherlock*. My second oldest brother Faisal was deep asleep after another graveyard shift the night before. My third oldest brother Kamal was at his security job. Aden was out doing whatever he did with his friends during this hour. Lastly, *Aabo* was at 52nd street having his eight hour-long coffee session.

Last of all there was *Hooyo*. She was downstairs listening to *BBC* radio after making the day's lunch. Of course it was *baasto* - one of the only three things that were cooked in our home.

I was feeling pretty starved, but I'd grown sick of eating the same old same old. So I told myself I'd grab a sandwich across the street after finishing my schoolwork. My stomach began to grumble wildly at one point while tuning into my show. I decided I couldn't treat a necessity like food as a reward any longer. So I shut off my laptop, put my homework aside and grabbed my purse from under my desk.

I went across the room to my closet and reached for the stack of endless shawls at the very top. I settled for my favorite shawl, the plain black one with the tassels. It was the one I always opted on wearing despite how many times my friends shunned me because of it.

"That again? What's with you and the black, woman?" My childhood friend Hodo would tell me.

"Seriously. What do you have against color? What did color ever do to you?" My other friend Fartun would tease.

I'd take their comments in stride and keep wearing my black shawl. It was just too near and dear for me to despise, or discard. Rushing, I wrapped it around my head and pulled on a black cardigan. All the black would tone down the crazy color combination that was my *baati*.

Hooyo always warned me against wearing a *baati* outdoors. In her words it was like giving up on yourself and letting people know you no longer cared. According to *Hooyo*, appearance was one of the most important things for a young woman to maintain. It just so happened that I wasn't interested in getting dressed up to get a sandwich from across the street. People's judgments were the farthest thing from my mind when I was hungry. I closed my bedroom door behind me and sprinted downstairs. Reaching the bottom of the stairs I found *Hooyo* sitting on the couch with her hands raised over her face. Her back was shaking as she trembled with what could only be tears. I froze.

It had been the first ever time that I saw my mother cry. I didn't know what to do or say. The thought of giving her a comforting word was what I dreaded most. My dry throat grew even drier as I struggled to make sense of what I was seeing. She began exhaling with deep heavy breaths. Soft wails escaped her lips, her thick mahogany brown *garbasaar* concealing the space that was her eyes. The loud voices of men on the radio were playing in the background.

"Another blast…Al-Shabaab is taking credit…Peacekeepers are notifying the public to stay alert."

Feeling numb I set my hand on the rail of the stairs and leaned against it for support. I stood there speechless for what seemed like an eternity. My mother was crying before my eyes. I wondered if she had heard me or even knew I was there? In that instant I hated myself for feeling hungry. Why hadn't I just eaten the *baasto* earlier? What made me crave some stupid sandwich?

As the thoughts ran rampant in my mind realization struck hard. I knew I couldn't stand quietly any longer. I licked my lips and tried forming some words in my mind. After another moment's silence they poured out of me all at once.

"Hooyo…..Hooyo? Are you okay?" I asked, trying my best at sounding calm.

No response. *Why did I feel so entitled to receive one?*

I made my way over to my mother, with small steps. It was almost as if the gentleness I took in them would affect her in some way. I lingered over her frame for a long silent moment before sitting down and softly pulling my arm across her shoulder. In that moment she felt so cold and small to me. My arm shook along with her movement, as my mother shielded her eyes from me.

I just *held her.* I promised myself I would be there, be present, for her while she gave into whatever sorrow was eating its way through her. I told myself that was the most I could do. All of a sudden my thoughts became a jungle entwined with endless vines.

Why had *Hooyo* been crying? Was it something she heard on the radio that triggered it? Was it because of *Aabo?* Was it something he said? I wondered how he would find the time to say something offensive to her when he was gone for the entirety of the day. I sat there wondering as *Hooyo* cried hopelessly beside me.

I made a quick attempt to reach for my *Hooyo's* hand but she wouldn't pull it away from her face. It was like she was too embarrassed to show her tears, her one *weakness.* I understood it but hated that I had to. *Hooyo's* breathing returned to a normal pace and her weeping came to a swift stop. It was then that her hands finally fell from her face and her eyes became exposed to mine.

Looking back into her puffed and reddened eyes, I struggled for the right words to say.

Hooyo slipped her hand into mine and squeezed it gently. She blinked as she tried to fight back more tears. It was then that I noticed the dark

126

circles around her eyes and the wrinkles covering her cheekbones. She never looked as old to me as she did in that moment. She shook her head and pulled her hand away.

"*Hooyo*, why are you crying? Please tell me what's making you so distressed?"

Hooyo lifted her head and pulled her lips into a tight, forced smile.

"I was just asking myself something and I-...."

I kept my eyes glued to *Hooyo*, and nodded her on pleading with her to speak her thoughts aloud.

Hooyo shook her head once more and half smiled. "Oh Hafsay. Don't you see it?"

"See what *Hooyo*?" I questioned, utterly clueless.

"I'm no mother to you and I can never be called one. A true mother is a woman who is a teacher for her children. One who teaches them valuable things they can practice in life. A mother is the first teacher to her children. But what could an illiterate woman like me teach anyone? I've failed you and your brothers. All I've done is bring you into this world. I've never helped any of you survive in it."

Hooyo sighed as her soft smile grew into a deep-set frown. Tears began to cloud her face once more. I was dumbfounded by all that *Hooyo* said, but more than that I was pained. How could *Hooyo* believe she was irrelevant in any of our lives? How could she see herself in that way?

I took hold of each of her hands and kissed them.

"*Hooyo*, you have taught us. You teach us each and every day. One of the most important lessons in life: to be strong. Don't you see that *Hooyo*? Every day you work hard and you wake up the next day just to do it all over again. Words are nothing without action. Through your actions you have taught us to keep going and to never quit. *Hooyo*, the greatest teachers are those who don't allow their students to quit. And you've never quit a day in your life. You're so strong *Hooyo*. I see it in you everyday…especially when you beat Aden after a night out!"

Hooyo laughed, and pulled me into a tight embrace. I didn't let go of her and wouldn't dare to. Tears began to fill my eyes as I sat there holding the one person worthy of all my love and admiration.

My *Hooyo Macaan*.

AABO

A group of four walked out of the restaurant doors as the old heads began hollering over their game again.

I laughed as one of the men playfully swung his cane at his friend. Actually he may have been serious. Losing a game of *Laaduu* was no light matter for the group of regulars, who prided themselves in claiming the table at the back of the restaurant. It was right next to the restrooms and had room enough for six people. It was one of the older tables my cousin Zak had in the restaurant, long before the renovation.

He wanted to replace the old bench for something slicker and newer, but the old heads put up a big protest. Zak let them keep their spot, so long as they promised to not get too rowdy and cause a scene. They were proving to break that promise today, as they had most nights.

The restaurant doors swung open, and in came my best friend Liban, or Lee for short. As per usual, he was late. He shook some snow off the shoulders of his grey trench coat and wiped his boots against the welcome mat. He wore a large grin on his face as he coolly walked over to the register. I nodded at him and checked the time. Over an hour late. Real slick.

"Wassup bro? You coolin'?" he asked me, extending his hand. I reached out to shake it.

"Yeah, man. What's good with you?"

Lee sighed, tucking his gloves into his coat pockets.

"Nothin' much bro. Just cold as hell. It's four degrees out there. Four degrees! Man, I'm trying to go out to Cali for break. You down to come?"

I shook my head. "I can't bro. I gotta help out around here. Besides, I'm waiting to hear back from the university. The new semester is gonna start in two weeks."

"*In sha Allah* you do bro. One of us gotta get our degrees out here. You still trying to do engineering?" he asked as he bent over and set his arms across the counter.

"Something like that, but I might change it up. I just wanna transfer already."

Lee nodded. "I feel you."

The old heads began shouting again. Someone must have lost.

"You gonna handle that before someone loses their gums?" Lee asked as we turned in their direction.

I laughed. "Nah, they'll be alright."

Lee shot up and rubbed his stomach. "Damn. You know how it is though. My ugly sisters stopped cooking again, and *Hooyo* won't tell them anything. Ya'll got anything for a young brotha to eat?"

"Man, you stay hungry. We got some rice and chicken on the stove if you want it," I replied.

Lee nodded. "That'll do bro. Hook me up."

"I hope you're paying this time. My cousin wanted me to make sure I told you," I said, smiling.

130

Lee laughed, and then got serious. "Damn, is he around?"

"Nah man, but he will be. I guess this will have to be to go, then." He looked terrified.

Lee nodded. "Good looks bro. Hook me up this one time."

I laughed and went into the back to pull something together for him. I grabbed a takeout container from a bag on top of the fridge and began loading it with rice and chicken. I thought back to Lee's terrified face and chuckled. I was only messing around with him when I mentioned my cousin. He knew he had a meal waiting for him whenever he dropped by.

I grabbed a ripe banana from the countertop and a couple of mild *shidni* containers from the fridge.

Lee was talking on the phone by the time I got back. I set his food onto the counter, and when he wasn't looking, I added a couple dollars into the register. It was something I always did when he came to eat. Zak trusted me, and I didn't want him losing money on account of any freebie meals.

"I can make it up to you, *wallahi*." Lee was sounding desperate.

I watched in amusement. This had to have been another one of the girls he was chasing after. There were a lot of them, and unfortunately for him, they always put a quick end to his chasing.

"Okay, if that's what you wanna believe. As long as we can stay friends, I'm good," Lee said matter of factly.

I cracked up in laughter. Some of the old heads shot me an annoyed look, like I had been the loud one all along. I became serious then and

131

pretended to be busy with the register. Lee pulled his phone away from his ear and stared at it in disbelief.

"She just hung up on me."

"You're lying? Say *wallahi*?!" I asked, ready to lose it. Lee shook his head and stuffed his phone back into his pocket. He looked pretty hurt.

"Was she fine?" I asked, trying to stop myself from smiling.

Lee sighed. "Hell yeah she was! Would I be begging if she wasn't?"

"Sorry, man. I'm sure you'll find your *xaliimo* in due time. Stay patient. Stay thirsty. You want some water to go with that *bariis*?" I couldn't keep a straight face.

Lee shook his head. "Nah, bro, it's not funny. She really hung up on me. Damn. That's the first time, too."

I had a hard time believing that but didn't want to dig too deep into him. At that same moment, I saw my mother's older brother, *Abti* Zubeyr entering the restaurant with a couple of men I'd never seen before.

"Ay, bro, my unc is coming. Take your food and sit down," I advised to a shocked and dismayed Lee. I wasn't sure he had heard me. After a moment, he grabbed his food and sat at a table a few feet away from me. I put on a serious face as *Abti* Zubeyr and his group approached. I made it a point to show my mother's brother the most respect.

"*Assalamu allaykum Abti, se layahay?*" he asked, separating from his group.

"*Wa alaykum assalam, Abti. Fican. Reerka se yihiin?*" I asked, resting my hands at the edge of the counter.

He nodded. "Alhamdulilah. Good - good. Listen, these are some men from outside the city. Let's try showing them a good time, huh?"

I smiled. "*Haa Abti*, I'll be sure to. What can I get you all?"

He briefly peered at the menu and to the back at the noisy group playing *Laaduu*. They were gonna be at it all night.

"Whatever they're having. It must be some good stuff."

I laughed. "Okay. The *shaah*, and what else?"

"*Bariis* and *hilib adhi*. We'll have two large plates. Add some bananas and *maraq*, as well. Oh, and a salad. One of these guys is a vegetarian," *Abti* said. He looked at me for a moment before we both erupted into loud laughter.

I shook my head. "He won't be for long. Our *hilib* is the best in town. I'll have it out for you in a minute, *Abti*."

"Thanks, *Abti*. Keep up the good work." He knocked on the countertop twice and rejoined his group of friends.

I watched him as he went off and shot Lee a look. He was going in on that *bariis* like it was his one-and- only solution to heartbreak. I almost wanted to record him, it was so hilarious.

"Yo, Lee!" I let out a sharp whistle. He looked up to me and nodded. I waved him over, and he rose slowly with his food in hand.

"I need your help getting some food ready. Are you done eating yet?" I looked down at the container in his hand. He had to be done.

"Yeah, man. What we doing?"

I had him follow me to the back. He hardly stopped eating but eventually did when I turned around to face him.

"My unc and his group want some *bariis* and *hilib adhi*. Problem is, there isn't enough of either." I said, breaking the bad news to him.

Lee wiped some grease from his mouth. "Damn, really? Well, what are you gonna do?"

I sighed and pulled out my wallet. "I'm gonna need you to run down to the spot across the street. I hear their *hilib adhi* is always on point. Get four plates of rice and two plates of *hilib*."

Lee started cracking up. "You gotta be kidding me man?!"

"*Wallahi*, I'm being serious. I tried getting my cousin to store up for next week, but he never wants to. So everything runs out early. What other option do I have?" I asked, frustrated.

Lee pulled himself together. "I guess this is it. Let me get that money. So, am I gonna be sneaking in through the backdoor or something, on some *James Bond* type shit?"

I smiled. "Yeah something like that. Just make sure you have everything with you."

"I got you, bro. I guess I'm gonna try spitting game to the girl working there. Think she's into dark guys?" He was grinning from ear to ear.

"Wow, you know how to jump back quick. Just make sure you get the food, bro." I patted him on the back as I walked past him.

Lee laughed and left from the back door. He came back in a second later. "You know somethin'? I hate the damn Midwest. My African ass ain't made for this snow. I swear I'm moving to Cali with my cousins."

"Whatever you say, bro," I muttered, leaving the kitchen area. Abti was seated at a table not too far from the *Laaduu* crew. He and his group were all speaking in low voices. I wondered what they could be talking about.

My snooping was interrupted by the sound of a text message. My step dad, Ilyas. He wanted me to know he'd be coming in an hour with a group of friends. As badly as I wanted to tell him to eat elsewhere, I didn't. I just hoped they wouldn't be in the mood for *bariis* and *hilib* like Abti was. I replied back to his text and hit send.

As soon as I did, I received another message. It was from Lee this time.

"Bro, I think she likes me. She won't stop staring, *wallahi.*" I laughed to myself and got ready to respond. That's when *Abti* called out to me.

"Yasin! *War* Yasin, *kaale!*"

A ball of anxiety hit me as I thought about Lee waiting on the orders. How was I going to explain this to him? I walked slowly over, anticipating the angry response I'd receive. It was going to be so embarrassing.

"We were just talking about your father," *Abti* said.

I held up my phone, breathing a sigh of relief. "I was just speaking to him now. He should be coming in an hour with friends."

Abti shook his head. "No, *Abti*. Your real father."

I froze, at a loss for words. Why was he mentioning him all of a sudden? And what did they have to say about him? One of the men next to *Abti* cleared his throat to speak.

"He was sponsored to come to the country. He's living in Minneapolis now."

Confused, I looked to my *Abti* for some type of clarification. Could this be true? It couldn't be. But why would they lie about something like this?

Abti nodded, looking to the man and then me. "It's true, he's here. Word is he's living with a group of men over in Riverside. I don't mean to surprise you, boy. I just thought it's important you know, before you go hearing it for yourself..."

I stepped away, confused. I hadn't heard from my dad since I was born, and now he was here, living in the same state as me. It was too much to take in.

"How long?" I asked, finally bringing myself to speak.

Abti turned to the men. "Months."

I nodded and headed towards the kitchen.

"Yasin," *Abti* said, forcing me to remain put.

"I want to be the one to tell your mother. You don't have to say a word, " he explained.

"Okay," I muttered as I walked back into the kitchen. My mind was racing with my emotions running wild. I tried imagining my *Aabo* living with a group of other men. He had been here all along, and I hadn't even known it. I messaged Lee and asked what the holdup was. I was going to kill him if he was flirting with that girl.

He messaged me back and said he was on the way. I went over to the sink and splashed some cold water over my face. I thought of my step dad coming here in an hour. Lee still away with the food and my dad here in the very same state as me. I could get to him in an hour's time. A man I hadn't seen since I was born. Now, the only thing separating us was a freeway and some traffic.

The only picture I had of him came to mind. A man with a distant look in his eyes, covered in facial hair. In the photo there was a space between him and my mother. It had always bothered me. An obnoxiously long knock at the kitchen back door interrupted me from my train of thought. Lee appeared, holding up two bags.

He grinned. "And that's not all."

Suddenly indifferent to his presence, I went over to the fridge and pulled out a head of lettuce. I grabbed the cutting board and a large knife and began cutting away.

"I wasn't lying about old girl. Bruh, she gave me her number!" Lee exclaimed.

From the corner of my eye I could see him setting the bags down and inching closer to me.

I stopped cutting for a moment and met his blank stare. "Thanks," I muttered.

Lee shrugged. "It's all good homie. So what's up? The old heads get pissed at you? Y'all should get rid of their table for good."

I sighed as I set my knife down and moved away from the uneven chunks of lettuce strewn across the surface of the cutting board. Lee narrowed his eyes at me, confused.

"What's up bro? Is everything good?"

"My dad - the real one - is here. In Minneapolis. He's been here for months now," I said, suddenly numb to the strange words I had heard only moments ago.

Lee widened his eyes as his mouth fell open. "For real?" I was pacing around the kitchen unknowingly while I said it.

Lee grabbed my arm suddenly, "Yasin?"

"Yeah, man. I'm serious. He's over at Riverside living with some other guys," I added, avoiding eye contact. My skin went cold remembering the picture again. *Hooyo's* stomach was big with Fuad, my oldest brother. So why had he looked so angry? Why the distance?

"That's crazy, bro. Does your moms know?"

I hadn't even stopped to think about *Hooyo*. How would this make her feel? Shocked and hurt, I imagined. She'd been the one to raise two boys alone in a whole new country. Without a doubt, she'd be the most affected by this news.

"Nah, not yet she doesn't," I replied as Lee watched me with close eyes.

"So what's the plan?" he asked, forcing my attention to the present.

"I don't know yet. Let's get these orders out first," I said.

"Grab the ranch and tomatoes. They wanted a salad, too."

****

At closing time Lee insisted he stick behind and help me clean up. This was a first for him.

I walked out of the back room and tossed Lee a towel. He caught it and began spraying the glossy mahogany table tops. I reached for my own bottle and began on the right side of the room. I wouldn't worry myself with mopping the floor since it'd been washed a few nights ago. There was too much on my mind, and the hardwood still looked to have a polished finish.

"What about this ugly thing?" Lee pointed towards the wooden bench top the old heads called their second home.

I shrugged. "Same difference, just spray it."

While I cleaned I thought about *Aabo*, living out in Riverside. He was going from one rough home to another. A part of me wished he could afford to live someplace better and not settle for the South Side.

Lee pulled out a chair and bent down to retrieve something. "What the hell?"

I looked over to him. "What's that?" With a confused expression he held up what looked like a crumpled dollar bill, only it wasn't very green. "Oh, that's a shilling!"

"The hell is a shilling?" he asked, looking at the bill strangely. I was almost positive he had never seen one in his life. My stepdad, Ilyas, would get a good laugh from this kind of thing. He called people my age the "*wallahi* generation", and shamed us for being out of touch with our culture. Lee was living proof of that.

I laughed. "It's Somali money. That's *Oday* Guled's, old dude with the cane. I can't believe he forgot it. He calls it his good luck charm." Lee laughed and dropped it onto the counter.

"Good luck, how? We're living in America. Old head needs to be carrying around a Benjamin."

I shook my head and began wiping the frames on the right side of the room. There were paintings of camels, livestock, nomads, and an old map of Somalia. The black frames were a good look against the dark red wall and hardwood floor. Something about it all just came together nicely.

"So, you cool with your pops?" Lee asked as he smoothed the creases out from the bill.

"He left after I was born. All I have of him is an old picture."

Lee sighed. "Damn, that's trippy. Your pops did ya'll grimy."

"Something like that. I just don't know how to feel about him...here all of a sudden. It's weird."

"Yeah, I feel you. You moms' tell you anything about him? What was he like?" He had never seemed so interested before. It was a refreshing change.

"She never had a lot to say about him. Just that he was quiet and was a part of the military in Somalia, before the war started."

Lee nodded. "Ay, that's what's up. My old man was a tailor in *Xamar*, had his own shop and everything. But don't tell anyone I told you that. He thinks he's hard now."

I sighed. "I always wondered what it would be like growing up with him in my life. A father figure.

Once I got a little older my mom married Ilyas. He's the closest thing I've got to a dad now."

"That's some *Jerry Springer* type - ay, my bad man. I ain't trying to be insensitive," Lee said seriously.

I shook my head. "It's cool man. I don't really mind."

Lee cleared his throat. "Bro I got some homies who live over in Cedar. If you want, we could come through and I don't know...maybe ya'll can meet."

I laughed. "What? Why would I do that?"

Lee sighed. "I don't know, so you can get some...what they call that shit?"

"Closure?" I said.

Lee nodded. "Yeah! You said you never met him. Now's your chance."

"I don't know, bro. I don't think I'm ready to. Besides, he walked out on us - why would I bother?"

"Yeah, but he is your dad. So I mean...just think about it. It ain't gotta be right this moment," Lee said.

I nodded, and stopped wiping to look out at the falling snow. Today was supposed to be one of the coldest days of the year. I wondered how *Aabo* was adjusting. Maybe he felt homesick every now and then. He probably craved the sun back in Somalia.

****

That night I came home to my mother, stepdad, and *Abti* Zubeyr sitting in the living room together. Once I connected the dots it was my mom's face that I looked to. She seemed distant.

"*Assalamu allaykum.*" I said.

"*Wa alaykum assalam.*" My *Abti* and Ilyas replied in matched unison. There was no response from *Hooyo*.

"*Hooyo, se tehay?* Are you doing okay?" I asked, coming to her side. Ilyas got up from beside her and made room for me to sit down. The tea in front of her hadn't been touched.

She didn't blink. "*Fican, Hooyo.* How was work?"

I nodded. "Good, and how was your day?"

"*Alhamdulilah,*" was her only response. I turned to *Abti* who was nodding and looking downward. Ilyas reached past me for his cell phone on the table.

"There's someone I need to call," he said, pulling his phone up to his ear and leaving the room.

I sighed and turned to *Hooyo*, stroking her back. "Do you know now too?"

"*Haa.*" She replied, glancing at her brother. *Abti* Zubeyr bit his lip and rubbed his hands together.

"How about Fuad? Did you tell him?" I turned to the both of them for an answer.

"No but he won't care all the same." *Hoyoo* muttered in response.

I leaned back in my chair and thought of Lee's offer to me. He had connections in Cedar and could easily find out where my dad was living. It was my choice to go or not.

"Your father is faring well. That's what I've told your mother. He's working in a restaurant, just like you."

142

I turned to *Hooyo*, feeling relieved. It was comforting to know he wasn't alone and supporting himself too. As a refugee he could have easily applied to receive benefits and get hand outs.

"Do you know the name of the restaurant?" *Hooyo* asked. I sat up and looked at *Abti* expectantly.

He met my eyes only for a second and shook his head. I wondered if he had actually known and was intentionally keeping it from *Hooyo*. We both knew how sensitive she could be with these types of things.

Ilyas returned to the living room with a big grin and realizing the nature of the gathering got serious.

"So what have we all decided to do?"

Abti sighed as he rose. "Oh I don't think we'll be discussing that now. I took enough of everyone's time tonight. I think I should be getting home."

"But you just got here?"Ilyas interjected. I sat on the edge of my seat.

Abti set a hand on Ilyas's shoulder. "We'll see each around *in sha Allah*. I'm sure of that."

Ilyas laughed heartily and shook my uncle's hand. "I've been meaning to ask you something. Let's walk out together."

Abti walked off with him and then stopped. "*Haye*, Hamdi. Get some rest and don't worry so much. He's doing well."

"*Haye, habeen wanaagsan.* " Hoyoo muttered tiredly.

Ilyas pulled his arm over *Abti* and led him towards the door. Disappointed, I realized I missed my chance to speak to *Abti* alone. He

143

seemed to know a lot about my father. If I was ever going to set out and meet him then he'd be the one to speak to.

Hooyo seemed lost in her own thoughts, staring blankly ahead. She would be like this for some time. Thoughts of the past always made her this way.

I reached out for her hand and squeezed it under my own.

"Everything is gonna be okay."

Hooyo nodded. "*In sha Allah*", she whispered in a weak mumble. I thought of *Abti* leaving and my missed opportunity to get some information about *Aabo*. I didn't want to leave *Hooyo* alone with her thoughts but she hadn't been the only one with a lot on her mind.

I shot up and fetched the *tusbaax* from across the table, handing it to her.

"*Hooyo*." I said. Her eyes fell over the green and black beads.

She smiled. "Verily in the remembrance of God do hearts find rest. My wise boy."

I grinned, "I just remembered I left something in *Abti's* car. I'll be back *Hooyo*."

Her smile quickly faded and her lips set into a tight frown.

"Be back soon. He's on his way home remember?"

"*Hayeh, Hooyo!*" I called out as I made a quick dash through the living room and over to the door. I ran as fast as my legs could let me and met Ilyas and *Abti* outside. By the time I reached them I was panting.

144

They both gave me strange looks, turning to one another. Lucky for me, *Abti* had still been around and seated in the driver's seat of his car.

"What's wrong?" Ilyas asked with a wide eyed stare.

I shrugged. "Nothing. I just needed to get something from *Abti* is all."

Ilyas shook his head and chuckled. "It must be something important. You look like you're about to pass out. *Haye* Zubeyr, take care of yourself. *Habeen wanaagsan!*"

I looked up at *Abti* but he didn't seem to notice. Ilyas patted my shoulder as he walked past me. *Abti* didn't waste any more time and switched on the engine of his car. He adjusted his mirrors and looked ready to drive off any second.

"*Abti!* Wait!" Nearly out of breath I ran over to his window.

He turned his head to acknowledge me and sighed. "What is it?"

I rested my right hand over the roof of his car and leaned in closer to speak.

"It's about my dad."

Abti shook his head. "I told you everything I know. I haven't got the time for this boy."

"Please," I pleaded with him. "I need to know where it is he works. I saw your face back in there. You didn't want my mother to know but you've got the name. You must have it."

Abti looked closely at me and then killed his engine. "You're as stubborn as he is. I'll give you that. What difference would it make to you?"

145

"A big difference *Abti*. He's still my father and it's important I try to go see him."

Abti shook his head and waved his hand dismissively. "No, absolutely not. Your mother would never allow you to."

I took a hold of *Abti's* arm. "It's my right and my own mother can't deny me that *Abti*."

He sat still and took a deep breath, before looking in the direction of my mother's house. I was still as he shook his head a few times and rubbed his eyes.

"It's just near Riverside. They call it *Bismillah Baasto and Bariis*. It's an older place," he finally told me.

I burst into laughter once I heard it and tried to regain my cool. *Abti* groaned.

"Is that really the name?" I asked, barely holding myself back from laughing in his face.

"Yes, now is that all you'd like me to answer. Or is there more?" *Abti* was impatient now.

"No, that's all *Abti*. Thank you. I appreciate it." I told him, feeling a weight lifted off my shoulders.

"Yeah, okay," he muttered, while he turned his attention to his mirrors.

"And when are you planning to make the trip?" I moved away from his car and looked up, like the answer was written somewhere in the night sky.

"I don't know. I'm not too sure yet," I replied, as he continued to fiddle with his mirror.

"Well don't tell your mother I told you anything. I don't want her blaming me for any of this. Understood?"

I nodded, "*Heya Abti*, it's clear. Thank you again, really. You've helped me a lot."

"Alright, get back inside before things start to look suspicious. She's probably already wondering and that's no good for her. We both know that."

All of a sudden I extended my hand out to him. "Thank you *Abti*."

"You're welcome boy. Now go. Get inside," he said sternly. I nodded and did as he asked me to.

When I got back inside the vibe seemed to be a little less tense. A classical Somali song played in the distance, while the air grew thick with sweet incense. I peeked into the living room to see Ilyas speaking softly to *Hooyo* and holding her hands. Something he said was making her smile and for that I was thankful.

I made my way up the stairs, digging through my jeans pocket for my phone. When I got it out I messaged Lee and told him to speak to his connections.

"Get some answers by tonight. We're leaving tomorrow."

I sent the message and tucked my phone back into my pocket. My brother's snores were the first thing to greet me when I got upstairs. It wouldn't be long before sleep called my name too.

****

After putting another twenty dollars in the register I surveyed the room. There weren't very many customers around but I knew that would change once the evening hit. Lucky for me I had spoke to my cousin this morning and told him I'd be taking off early. He hadn't minded and said he'd have one of his friends come in once I left. Lee came early this time around and was scrambling in the kitchen for something to eat. He was taking advantage of the short time the cooks would be in the prayer room, offering *Asr*.

I could hear the fridge rattling behind me and the sound of a soda can being opened. That's when I noticed Faisal, one of the older cooks. He was leaving the prayer room and heading towards the dining hall.

"Yo! Lee!" I called out, looking over my shoulder. In the next second he was sprinting out of the kitchen entrance, carrying a bag low enough to touch the ground.

"Damn they back already?" Lee ducked his head and looked around.

"You had like six minutes. What were you in there so long for?" I looked at the black bag taking a guess at what could be inside. There must have been a couple of bananas in there from the looks of it.

"Just a little something. Ya'll aint got a whole lot back there today. Who eats all that soup anyway?" He sounded annoyed.

I sighed. "Forget that. Did you hear back from anyone?"

"Nah man not yet. I sent out the message last night too. It's whatever we still going. You know the name of that restaurant don't you?" Lee tried concealing the bag behind his back. I nodded.

"Then we good. It's a weekday so he probably working over there anyway. We could check and see regardless," Lee explained, tapping his knuckles against the countertop.

"That's a really good idea actually." I said looking at him a little surprised. Lee was no Einstein but every now and then he shocked me with a brilliant idea. He smiled satisfied, looking like he was proud of himself.

"You know you didn't have to get all that. We could've stopped by a gas station somewhere." I told him, looking at the badly hidden bag of food.

Lee shrugged. "You did say it was a road trip homie. A bag of chips ain't gonna hold me that long."

I laughed. "Yeah but raiding the fridge ain't helping us either."

"It's all good bro. I got ya'll when I make it big *in sha Allah*. I'll write your unc a fat check and get this place on the map. Just watch," he said running his hand through his curly head of hair.

"*In sha Allah*, we'll see about that," I replied. One of the old heads was shouting about something again, and that's when I remembered the crumpled bill Lee found the other night. I turned to him all of a sudden. "You still have that shilling?"

Lee blinked. "A what-what? Yo bro you gotta be speaking English at all times."

I sighed. "The money you found on the floor last night. You got it on you?"

"Ohh THAT!" Lee exclaimed. "Nah man I threw it at a dude sitting on the curb this morning."

"You what?! Bro that's Somali money! What the hell is he gonna do with that here?"

Lee laughed. "Chill, the dude *was* Somali. He got laid out this morning by my boy. Talking too much trash. So I threw the money at him. I told his ass to go back to Somalia and find-"

"Good afternoon gentlemen." A middle aged White man in a blue and black winter coat said, approaching the register. Lee stopped telling his story as we both turned in his direction.

"What's your special of the day?" he asked smiling.

Lee stepped up to the register. "Hello there sir. Our special of the day is an amazing stew. The locals call it *maraq* and it's a hot Somali flavored broth you won't be able to get enough of. I guarantee it!"

I couldn't contain my laughter and turned towards the wall, pretending to look interested at the menu. There was always that one *Ajnabi* person that came to the restaurant and Lee was always of great service to them. Taking their orders was one of his favorite things to do when he came by the restaurant.

"That sounds marvelous. I'd love to try that. Does it come with any kind of special bread?" The man asked intrigued. I turned to look at him to see his eyes glued to Lee like he was hypnotized. Lee could be a smooth talker when he wanted to be.

"It sure does. You can have it with *malawax* or what you know as crepes, flat bread, or *jabaati*. That's a bit like naan bread but only sweeter," Lee replied. I covered my arm over my mouth and went into the kitchen to laugh out loud. He was by far the funniest when he pulled on this character. He made sure the *Ajnabi* customers always left happy and appreciative of the restaurant and service. They posted their good reviews online too and it was all thanks to Lee.

"I'll have it with the naan bread, thank you. How much will that be?"

"Dollar a piece but I'll make it fifty because I like your energy," Lee said grinning.

****

We hit the freeway after stopping at a gas station in our neighborhood. It was going to be an hour long drive but probably more with all the traffic lining up the road. Lee was driving there and lucky for me he could get there fast. He had made the trip six times before.

I glanced away from the maze of cars ahead of me and went over what I'd say to *Aabo*.

I always imagined we'd see each other on our own terms and not by my own choosing. I imagined my brother Fuad would be disappointed with me. He never liked to talk or hear about *Aabo*. In his eyes he completely betrayed us and didn't have a right to be known as our father. I understood his feelings to some extent. Growing up I had always felt sorry for Fuad. Shouldering the responsibility of my father was no easy task.

Fuad's middle and high school years were dedicated to working and taking care of *Hooyo* and me. I always told myself his hatred for *Aabo* must've come from the pain of his early years being stolen from him. It was only in college when he'd gotten a break with Ilyas coming into the picture and helping pay most of the bills. *Aabo* had done more damage than good and yet here I was making an hour long trip to see him. I just hoped he wouldn't turn me away and act like our relationship didn't matter to him.

I looked over to Lee, who was rapping along to a song blasting from his stereo. It was something about having fake friends and haters. I'd already gotten used to the noise level in his car and had no trouble drowning it out when I needed to. Lee bounced his head along to the

151

tune and threw up his hands when the chorus played. He noticed me staring and laughed hysterically.

"My bad bruh! I get caught up in it sometimes." Lee reached over to lower the volume.

"You're good man. So any of your boys in Cedar hit you up yet?" I asked, as he veered into the right lane.

"Oh-damn almost caught a bumper. Nah man none of em. But you good bruh, you got me."

"It's cool man. We can go to the restaurant like you said. If he ain't there we'll just dip," I said looking forward again. Nothing but flashing car lights were ahead of us.

"Word? I mean we could always get a PI and just hire him to watch old head. Be hella funny to get a report back from him," Lee said chuckling. "He'd be like-"sir your father's always loitering around in Cedar. It's as if he knows the whole neighborhood."

I shook my head, laughing. "Nah man that's not necessary. We'll do our own investigating."

Lee turned to me. "So whatchu got on your mind bruh?"

"Nothing man. I'm just cooling." I shrugged like everything was okay.

Lee sighed. "Nah be real with me man. What's up?"

I hesitated and then finally hit him with the truth.

"What am I even gonna say to him? Yo I'm your son and you left my mom's but I heard you're here now and I just wanted to meet you."

"Just be real. That's your pops man. Tell him how you feel," Lee said. I felt my stomach tighten on me.

I shook my head, protesting. "Nah Lee, we're men. We don't talk about our feelings. He'll just think I'm hella soft."

Lee sighed. "Really bruh? Cmon now. That's some bull and you know it. Open up to him. I know it sounds weird but that's the only way bro."

I sighed, laughing. "Man you know what I'm saying is true. Put yourself in my shoes. Imagine if you did what you told me to." I turned to Lee for an answer.

He was quiet for what seemed like a full two minutes. I laughed. "Yeah exactly."

"No not exactly. I'm just trying to imagine what that would feel like. *Alhamdulilah* my pops is in my life but damn if he wasn't...I don't know what I'd be like."

"You'd still be Lee. What do you mean?"

Lee shuffled around in his seat. "I don't know. I guess he influenced me and all that. Been there to talk to me and help me out. My pops is a G *wallahi*. That's a fact."

I lowered my eyes and tried to stop from feeling jealous. It was true. Lee's dad had always been there for him. I knew because I was there to watch and wish I had that same support in my life. The closest I ever got to having that was through Ilyas but he was only my step dad.

Lee cleared his throat. "It's whatever though cuz *Allah* would still have my back. I mean look at you. You're doing way better than me."

"What do you mean better?"

Lee shrugged. "You got brains brotha! I dropped out of school and you're headed to university. You got a job and I don't. Only thing I have is this whip and it ain't even all that."

"Lee-c'mon bro. Chill," I said getting serious. "That doesn't mean anything. You can go back to school and find a job just as fast. Quit playin."

Lee laughed out loud. "Yeah man I know. I'm just sayin'. Having a dad doesn't make or break you. And if he's not interested in talking that's cool too. Cuz he was never there from the start."

I nodded. "You're speaking facts bruh. Good looks."

"I gotchu' bruh," Lee said, while looking over his shoulder to change lanes.

"I appreciate it bro. And you're right, if he's not having it we'll just dip. That doesn't change anything."

Lee nodded. "Exactly bro. That's one hunnit'."

"I got the rest of the day off from work. So we'll just chill around the city. I haven't been back in a minute," I said, leaning back into my seat. The sun was hitting my side of the window, so I covered my hand over my right eye.

"Me neither," Lee replied.

I tried loosening my body up but felt my hands begin to shake. I clamped them together as the sweat began to grow sticky in my palms. Lee started singing along to something again.

I asked myself if I would really care. Working up the confidence to speak to *Aabo* was one thing and accepting rejection was another. I prayed he wasn't anything like Fuad made him out to be.

Just like I was taking a chance to see him today, I hoped he'd be equally as open to talk to me.

****

The clock hit seven when we reached South Side Cedar. Everyone and their momma had been out and about. There were more people walking then cars on the street. I let my eyes dance around from one corner shop to another. *Asad's Restaurant. Halima's Halal Meat. Safari Cell Phone Repair.*

There were bumper stickers with mini Somali flags and Islam means peace, in place of the usual coexist ones. Women were wearing bright colored *jilbabs* that brushed against the ground. Parked taxi cars filled the street sides while groups of men my age conversed outside restaurant doors. Little Mogadishu hadn't changed one bit.

It had been years since I'd been back and everything and everyone seemed all the more interesting to me. Every late middle aged man caught my attention a second longer, while I secretly wondered if they could be *Aabo*. For all I knew he could have been strolling the sidewalks or huddled in a circle outside of a corner store. The idea of seeing him made the anxiety I felt explode like fireworks in my stomach.

Lee lowered the volume of his car stereo, "Shit is alive tonight." I sat up as my eyes darted from side to side.

"East Lake Street. It should be right next to-"

"Bro I remember. You told me like ten times. I got it memorized now! East Lake Street 1300."

I laughed nervously. "Yeah just reminding you."

"Hey relax man. It'll be chill. Keep it positive. It's all about the law of attraction. You remember that?" He reminded me. It had been his latest obsession and all he could talk about.

"Yeah I know," I muttered turning to look at the older men crossing the street by the repair shop. One of the men wearing an untucked white shirt underneath his jacket locked eyes with me and for a second I convinced myself it was him. When we drove past the group I found myself turning back to look at him.

"I'll pretend to order and you take a look around. He might be serving, maybe even cooking. Get up to use the bathroom and just go back there to see." Lee was saying this while my heart pounded in my chest. I wondered if it would stop beating then. Would I even make it there alive?

"I know it ain't supposed to be for real but you think we can order a plate of something? I got the munchies *wallahi*. I could eat a whole goat right now." Lee sighed.

"Yeah man whatever," I said while crossing my hands over my stomach. I felt a little queasy.

Lee looked at me. "You good bro? We can pull over if you want. I don't want any accidents in my car."

"I'm good. Just keep driving."

I could see Cedar Riverside in the distance, the most notable part of the Minneapolis skyline. The sky high grey apartment buildings that so many Somalis living in South Side called their home. I would have never expected *Aabo* to be one of them.

For a second I told myself Lee may have been right. I was starting to feel a little sick. Just as he made a sharp right turn into a narrow street a strange feeling hit my stomach. I knew it was coming any minute now.

"Pull over!" I shouted as loud as I could manage. Lee was still driving through the intersection.

"What? Right now?!" He asked bewildered. I leaned forward and gripped my right arm over my stomach and used my left to shield whatever wanted to fly out of my mouth.

"Now!" I exclaimed. The greasy fish steak I had for lunch was begging to come out.

Lee quickly veered to the right side of the road and parked alongside a green and white building. I ran out of the car and over to the closest trash can I saw. Out it came in varying chunks of brown and green. Lee bolted out of the driver's seat and looked over at me.

Two older women in matching black *jilbabs* passed by me and clicked their tongues in distaste.

"Disappointing. Another drunk in the neighborhood." One of the women said.

"What a shame." The other spat, with complete disgust.

"His mother outta chuck him back to Somalia. That'll fix him."

I didn't pay them any attention and wasn't sure Lee had heard them. They were nearly gone when Lee stepped up all of a sudden. "Hey mind your own business! He's not your son!"

"Go lecture your own damn kids!" The Somali he was speaking didn't miss a beat.

I smiled, wiping my mouth dry. The women hurried past me once they noticed me backing away from the trash can. Lee roared with laughter, unable to stand up straight.

"Welcome to Cedar fam!" He proclaimed, raising his hands out in the air. I pretended to stumble back to the car and got back inside. Lee laughed, hopping back in himself.

"What is it about this place?" He said, a wide smile filling his face. "For real man."

I looked at him for more explanation. There was still a nasty taste of puke in the back of my throat. So I dug into my pocket and pulled out some mints.

He sighed. "Something about this town *wallahi*. It feels right...like home."

"Home?" Lee was losing me now.

He shrugged nonchalant. "This is what it must be like in Somalia. I know I always be trashing it but sometimes I wish I was there."

"Yeah man same here. It must be the vibes," I added looking around at the people filling the sidewalks. Somali names written on nearly every business, faces of people who could be your own brother or mother. It had felt like home.

Lee started up his engine. "You feel okay though? Think you can make it there alright?"

I nodded. "Definitely man." Lee pulled into the road and continued down the Cedar streets.

"We need to come down here more often. I missed this place," Lee said racing through a yellow light.

"Yeah," I muttered, lowering my window to get a feel of the cool night's air.

Lee shook his head. "They wanna tear it down."

I looked ahead to the infamous Riverside complex. Its multi colored blue and red windows, the height of it nearly reaching the heavens. I was in awe.

"It's an eyesore. Screw them! That's our place. I won't let them touch it," Lee said, with a shaky voice.

I looked at him then. He seemed to finally look his age for once. Twenty years old, just like me. Even though anyone else could easily mistake him for older. Growing up in South Side must have matured him more than I'd like to think. He called this town home once and never wanted anyone to forget it.

His growling stomach broke the moment's silence. I laughed, thankful the vibe had changed.

"I told you I was hungry bro! I need to eat every hour minimum," Lee complained.

"But where does it all go? You're bony as hell," I replied laughing to myself. Lee chuckled, rubbing his stomach.

"I was a fat kid man, you didn't know? Everyone used to bully me at *dugsi*. Now it's all muscle, *Alhamdulilah*." He smiled, flexing his left arm.

"Ain't nothing there! For real," I joked. He showed off his left bicep in different angles.

Lee grinned. "You stay hating man, just don't be surprised when I get bigger than *The Rock*. Your boy is gonna be ripped soon."

I smiled to myself as my eyes flashed over a restaurant we drove past. There was a sign in bright orange letters reading, "*Bismillah Baasto and Bariis.*" I slowly leaned forward as I switched my head left for a double take.

"It's there bro! You just missed it!" I hollered.

All of a sudden Lee veered to his left and then made an illegal u turn causing a car to honk for what seemed like a lifetime. He ignored their loud beeps and drove slowly past the side of the road we passed before.

"Just park anywhere. I know I saw it here." I was close to jumping out of the car in my excitement.

"Calm down bro," Lee said, grabbing a hold of the wheel with both hands.

He'd never drove like that in his life. After going at a snail's pace for a few minutes he finally parked alongside the curb. I raced out of the car not bothering for him to kill his engine at all. Soon Lee joined me, locking his car after him. I walked slowly past the shops and centers, searching for the bright orange letters I'd seen earlier. Lee sped over to catch up to me and pulled up his pants.

"Where'd you say it was?" He asked looking at the businesses all around us.

I ignored him and stared at every shop and restaurant. I knew it had to be here somewhere.

Almost ready to give up, I stopped in front of a mobile shop and noticed it from the corner of my eye. The restaurant was alongside it but nearly hidden from view. It was a literal hole in the wall.

"Right there!" Lee exclaimed. I didn't waste any time and headed inside.

The place was a lot bigger inside than what the outside portrayed it to be. There were a lot of men seated in groups, adding to the humid air in the room. It stunk of frying oil and goat meat.

"Damn they ain't got an AC?" Lee asked, looking to each side. I pulled myself towards the front of the room and dropped down into the first open booth. Everyone had been seated except for us and there were no servers in sight.

"Wow," Lee mumbled loud enough for me to hear. Secretly, we'd both been comparing it to my cousin's restaurant back home in St Cloud and judging it for all that it lacked. The smell of frying oil grew stronger. I felt myself growing more nauseas by the minute.

I looked around for any sight of him and tried to picture the old photo. The round nose that was like Fuad's, thin lips pulled tightly together and those eyes. I wouldn't be able to forget them. But every face I saw was nothing like the one I knew to be his.

"Should we go up and ask for service or what?" Lee asked, yawning.

I shook my head. "Nah let's just wait around. We don't need to get noticed yet."

My heart was close to jumping out of my chest any second now. Lee began tapping the table top adding to the anxiety creeping over me. *Where could Aabo be?* I looked from one group of men eating to the next. Lee sighed and pulled out his phone. I was starting to grow

161

hopeless and regretted ever having come down here. What were the chances I'd see him here anyway?

Lee sighed and set his phone onto the counter, "See him yet?"

"Nah," I muttered, meeting his eyes. "Think I should check the back like you said?"

"You could, but it doesn't look like they'll miss anything here," Lee muttered, turning to the group of men seated not very far from us. Some of them looked back at us with mistrusting expressions. He was right. They'd know something was up.

"What time is it?" I asked Lee, glancing at his phone on the table. I left mine charging at home again.

Lee picked it up. "Uhh seven thirty seven. You got some place else to be?"

"Nah, do you? We could leave right now," I said, glancing anxiously around the restaurant again.

Lee shook his head. "Bruh you good. We can wait around as long as you want."

I nodded and looked down. This was beginning to feel like one big waste of time.

He obviously wasn't around and we wasted an hour of our day to get here. Lee peered at something across the room. I looked back around to see it was the menu. He mentioned he'd been hungry while on the way here. Before I could suggest we order a short Somali man appeared in front of us.

"*Walayaal*, are you ready to order?" He asked, locking his hands together behind his back. A wash towel was hanging over his right shoulder and I could tell he'd been drying dishes earlier. Lee's face lit up with a smile. He'd been waiting to get asked that all night.

"I'll have a federation plate if you guys do that here. With *moos* and *shidni* on the side."

The man nodded and grabbed a pen from behind his ear. He began writing in a notepad he pulled out from his pocket. It was clear there were no menus, as was the case for most Somali restaurants in the Twin Cities. I'd just settle for something simple.

Once he finished writing he glanced over at me. "And what will you be having brother?"

I pulled my hands together. "I'll have some *bariis* with *hilib adhi* and *moos*. No *bisbaas* for me."

"*Heya*, and would you guys like anything to drink?" He asked, pulling his pen close to his notepad.

Lee leaned forward. "Yeah let me get an orange soda."

"Same for me thanks," I said. The man nodded and headed off towards the kitchen area.

Lee rubbed his hands together and licked his lips. "Your boy's gonna go in *wallahi*."

I half grinned. "It's been a minute huh?"

"What would you rate it?" Lee asked with smiling eyes, looking around the restaurant. I let my eyes wander myself. It wasn't the best looking

163

place you could eat. The walls were a boring pale beige, floors a chipped black and the chairs were old and worn.

"I'd give it a two and a half but I haven't tried the food yet." I answered, my eye catching onto the Somali and American flags pinned onto the wall.

Lee laughed. "Yeah that's true."

"Not everybody got funds like your cuz does," Lee said, with a smirk. I shrugged in response.

"Well that's only the icing on the cake. The food quality is what really matters," I said digging my hands into my pockets.

Lee nodded. "Bet. I hope they make a bomb *baasto*."

"I thought you ordered federation?" I asked confused.

"I did but the *baasto* is what makes or breaks it for me," Lee replied, while glancing ahead of him. He kept eyeing the main menu on the wall as if the food pictured were real. I imagined he was having the *hilib adhi* pictured next to the strawberry fruit smoothie in his mind.

"Yoooo! I got a message back!" Lee exclaimed jumping in his seat. I turned to my right as a group of men getting up to leave narrowed their eyes at us. One of the guys was glaring right at me.

"Ay keep it down man," I whispered, feeling embarrassed by his commotion. Luckily the group had left the restaurant along with their judgments of us. I looked back to Lee who's smile quickly turned into a frown. He lowered his phone and began shaking his head.

Lee groaned. "C'mon man."

"What's up?" I asked a little worried.

Lee sighed. "She gave me the wrong number."

"Who?" I asked. Lee scratched the back of his neck in contemplation. He looked hurt.

"The girl from the restaurant. One across the street from your uncle's. I thought she was feeling me *wallahi*." Lee stroked his chin as he kept his eyes lowered.

"Bro, c'mon now. There's way more girls out there for you. Besides she ain't even your type."

Lee laughed dryly. "I aint gotta type. Can't believe this. Some dude just texted me saying, "bro I'm a guy.""

I couldn't contain my laughter and fell back against my seat, hooting and hollering.

"You just gonna laugh at me? Wow. Some friend you are."

I cackled in delight and stopped to take a much needed breath. "Say *wallahi* he said that?"

Lee held up his phone. "I don't have to it's right here on my screen."

"Oh my goodness, bruh. You got played. Damn!" I said as my chest heaved up and down.

Lee narrowed his eyes at me. "At least I'm man enough to holler at a girl. When's the last time you got a chick's number? I'll wait."

"Nah homie. Don't try coming at me cuz you got rejected. Be man enough to accept it." Lee ignored me, and turned to look at his phone. He wasn't going to forget this one for awhile.

"Bro I was just playing. Don't be so sensitive all the time." I told him. He didn't bother to hear me out.

I sat back in my seat and waited for our food to arrive. It had been awhile now and we still hadn't even been served our drinks. This place was looking to get a bad review online. I was amazed at how full it was. Their customers must've had some low expectations. While I examined the restaurant a man appeared from the back with a large black tray. It was empty and he was holding it like a binder.

He moved to the center of the room and began stacking plates and cups onto it. I had my whole attention on him as he did it. There was either something very interesting about him, or I had been that bored. Once he finished collecting the dishes, he carefully grabbed the tray by the ends and walked back in the direction he came from. I hadn't gotten a good look at his face. *Aabo* was a lot thinner in the picture and this man was more round. I could imagine a weight gain as he aged but I still wasn't completely convinced it was him.

Lee stomped his feet against the ground like a bratty toddler.

"The service here is trash bro!"

Just as he said that the man from before appeared, who had taken our orders. Lee and I both sat up attentively. His forehead was drenched in sweat. "Sorry guys. It's taking a long time, huh?"

Lee sighed. "We got places to be man. What's the hold up?"

"I'm sorry. We were having some issues before but the food should be out soon. Excuse me," he said before rushing back towards the kitchen doors.

Lee breathed deeply, "What a night."

"Sorry bro. I didn't think it'd turn out like this. My bad."

Lee stroked his neck. "Nah bruh it's whatever. I just want my food already...wow. Now they bring us the water."

I turned around to see the man clearing the table before, appear with a tray of two cups and a pitcher of water. I looked closely at his face this time. His hair was receding and his eyes were narrowed, like he'd been trying hard to focus on something. The rest of his features didn't stand out very much to me.

"*Assalamu allaykum*. How are we doing tonight?" he asked, setting the tray down.

Lee sighed. "Hungry."

The man grinned with a tired look in his eyes. He didn't listen for my response but glanced at me when he set a cup by my side. I watched as he poured ice water into my cup and set the pitcher at the center of the table.

"If you need anything, I'll be around for the next twenty minutes," he said before walking off with his large black tray.

Lee grunted. "No thanks." He rolled his eyes as he took a sip of the water.

"It tastes alright. Try it." He took another sip. I looked back around for the man but he was nowhere in sight. I sat there and tried remembering his face and voice. Was there something I had missed? I forced the picture back into my mind but there was no connection.

"We should've just gone to a drive thru," Lee grumbled, while picking up his phone again.

I wished he'd just keep quiet while I gave it some thought. Was this man my father or not?

A pair of two older men walked in and took a seat at the table in front of us. They were speaking loud and that made it all the harder for me to think. I thought of leaving to the bathroom so I could get some peace and quiet. Maybe I would remember then.

"You right bro, she ain't even my type. I'm getting desperate these days...hollering at any girl," Lee said while scrolling through his phone. The men in front of us began laughing about something. I was starting to get annoyed by all the noise.

"She should be grateful I even tried talking to her. Ain't nothing special about her," Lee muttered with some venom in his voice. I turned my attention towards the opposite side of the room.

"We're ready to order!" One of the men called out. "Someone come over already!"

A moment after they said it the round man from earlier reappeared. He walked at a quick speed and came to their table. "You two again? Aah it's gonna be a long night."

The pair chuckled hard and soon the man joined in as well. I watched closely.

"How's your night going?" One of the men asked the waiter.

He sighed. "*Alhamdulilah* it wasn't so bad. I'm going home soon. So don't give me such a hard time."

"Miya? Okay then we won't. You look a little tired. Are you sure the work is going well?" The other man asked.

The waiter set his hand over his chest. "I'm still alive. So no complaints from me."

The other man laughed. "You're right. That's all that matters despite everything else."

"Try telling that to my wife. She thinks money grows on trees here. Everyday it's send us some money. Why have you forgotten your family?" The waiter complained, while still managing to smile.

"It's not an easy life but *Allah* didn't intend for it to be. You haven't been here long but you're doing well for yourself. How is it in Riverside?" One of the men asked.

I began connecting the dots. Feeling alert I looked towards Lee. He didn't seem to notice anything but whatever was on his phone. I peered back up at the group and listened.

"Not too bad. The Somalis make it seem like hell. I actually like it. It's heaven compared to back home. They shouldn't forget that." The waiter said. There was only one last thing I needed to hear to confirm any suspicion that I was having.

"I like you Hassan. You're a good man." One of the men said. "You're going to last here."

He smiled. "*In sha Allah*. I hope that's the case. So what can I help you both to?"

I couldn't peel my eyes away. There he was, standing a few feet away from me. My *Aabo*.

"My service is so whack. I need to change it up *wallahi*," Lee said under his breath.

He was shorter and wider than he'd been in the photo. His small afro was gone and all that remained was thin receding hair, tinted with grey at the sides. He looked nothing like he did before, but it was still him. Hassan Ali Sharif, *my Aabo*.

Lee sighed. "We should boycott this place. I hope they go out of business soon."

I lowered my eyes as *Aabo* walked past our table. A moment later our food was brought out to us. In a matter of seconds the table was filled with federation, rice, bananas, spice, and a large plate of salad. Lee loosened up now as he pulled the plate of federation closer to himself.

"The salad is our treat. Enjoy guys." The man with the towel said. He was joined by another man I hadn't seen before. They left us alone with the steaming hot food staring back at us.

"Yo where's our soda?!" Lee exclaimed. "Man whatever...I'm eating regardless."

Whatever appetite I had was gone and all I wanted to do was leave the restaurant. I finally realized how foolish I been. Of course *Aabo* would have remarried and had other kids. There was nothing stopping him from doing so and I was naive to think otherwise. Lee stuffed his face from one thing to the next. I left my food untouched. All I wanted to do was walk out and leave. Only Lee had been driving and I had no one else to take me back home. Besides I didn't want him to think something was wrong. I slowly grabbed my fork and forced myself to take a few bites of rice.

"It ain't all that bad," Lee said in between bites. "The *shidni* is hella hot though. Don't add too much."

I nodded as I chewed some of the rice. I reached across the table and added some salad on the side. As I ate in silence I saw my father reappear with another man. They were carrying two trays of food and drinks. I lowered my fork and watched from the distance.

Aabo smiled and set the tray of rice down, the other man doing the same. He leaned one hand against the wall as he spoke to the men. I thought of his new wife and children. *One boy, two girls? Three girls, two boys?* Lee reached across the table for napkins that weren't there.

I realized I wouldn't speak to him. He didn't have to know I was his son or that I travelled an hour just to come meet him. I didn't want to burden him in that way. *Aabo* playfully nudged the man standing next to him. His beard was gone and that made him look all the more unrecognizable to me. Fuad and he had shared the same laugh.

"At least we got water," Lee muttered, reaching to take a sip from his cup.

"Yeah, that's true," I replied, still watching closely over *Aabo*. Looking at the picture I would have never guessed him to be a man that could afford to smile or laugh. Yet here he was, easily doing both. I reached for my own water and took a sip. *Aabo* and the other man left the two men to eat. I quickly looked down as he walked past our own table.

"How's the food?" He asked smiling, standing over our table.

Lee stopped eating as I looked off to the side.

"Good! *Mahadsanid*," he happily replied for the both of us. *Aabo* gave a simple thumbs up and walked away. For a second I thought of telling

Lee and then thought better of it. He didn't need to know. It would be my own secret to keep.

"Sorry you didn't get to see your pops bro. We can come back," Lee said, with his mouth full.

A few pieces of food flew across the table as he spoke.

"Nah, man that's okay," I said solemnly.

"Whatchu mean? You don't want to meet him anymore?" Lee looked confused.

"Nah, it's just...I don't know maybe it's not meant to be." An hour ago I would've never thought I would say those words. Life was strange.

Lee shrugged."Alright man but let me know if you're down to do this again. I don't mind coming back."

I nodded and continued forking my food disinterestedly, while Lee went on eating. I would be lying if I said it didn't hurt. The pain was going to numb me for weeks and maybe even longer.

Aabo supporting another woman and kids stranger to me. I couldn't understand what was so wrong with *Hooyo*, Fuad and me. *Why hadn't he stayed by Hooyo's side and come to the country with us?* It was a lot less stressful than the life he was currently leading. As I thought about him more he reappeared again. He pulled on a black winter jacket as he passed our table once more. The two men in front of us stopped eating to speak to him. I watched the interaction with less interest than before.

"Enjoy your meal guys. If anything tastes bad make them give you a refund and just ask for more." *Aabo* said with a grand laugh. The two men chuckled.

172

"Heya, habeen wanaagsan." He said waving on his way out of the restaurant doors.

Had I made the best choice? I wasn't sure but my gut feeling was what ultimately made me keep silent. At the very least *Aabo* was alive, happy and healthy. He was working and living with other men, so he wasn't lonely either. In the end I was grateful to *Allah* that he'd been watching over him all this time. All of a sudden my phone vibrated with a text. It was from my stepdad Ilyas. I opened the message and read it. He wanted to know when I was coming home. Apparently *Hooyo* had been worried about me and he didn't want her to feel that way.

I looked at Lee, who ate away, oblivious to all that was around him.

"I'll be back soon *in sha Allah*. Tell *Hooyo* not to worry." I sent the response and took a deep breath.

I looked towards the restaurant doors and imagined *Aabo* walking down the snow covered streets. Everything here was foreign to him-including me. I guess my silence was for the best. *Hooyo* always said, *"af daboolan, dahab waaye."* She couldn't have been more right.

Glossary

Abaayo- 'Sister'

Abaya – Islamic women's dress, usually black, and loose fitting

Adhaan- Islamic call to prayer

Af daboolan, dahab waaye- Somali saying: a silent mouth is golden

Ajnabi- Non-Somali/foreigner

Allah- Arabic word for God

Allahu Akbar- 'God is great'

Alhamdulilah- All praise is to Allah

Ameen- Arabic for Amen

Aroos- Wedding

Asr- afternoon prayer (Islam)

Assalamu allaykum- Peace be upon you (Islamic greeting)

Awoowe- Grandfather

Bas- Enough/that's it

Baasto- Somali style pasta

Baati- Colorful cotton Somali dress worn by women

Bariis- Somali styled rice

Bisbaas- Spice

Bismillah- In the name of Allah (God)

Cadey- light skinned woman

Calaf- Destiny

Cirad Madoow- black gums (a sign of beauty)

Ciyaal suuq- (direct translation is kids of the market) i.e. misguided youth

Dambi- Sins

Dhax dhuuban- Small waist on a woman

Dirac- Somali dress worn for weddings

Dolsho- Somali traditional cake

Dugsi- Islamic studies school for children-specializing in Quran

Eid- Islamic holiday

Fadhi ku dirir- (direct translation is fighting while sitting) older men arguing about politics in coffee shops

Fanax- gap in the teeth (sign of beauty)

Federation- Somali dish consistent of pasta/rice/meat

Fiican se tahay- Good, how are you?

Garbasaar- Somali hijab word indoors (for prayer)

Haa- Yes

Habaryar- Aunt (Mother's side)

Habeen- Night

Haye- Okay

Hawalad- A center to send money back home (Somalia, Ethiopia, Kenya) to relatives

Hee- What?

Hijab- Islamic headscarf

Hilib adhi- Goat meat

Ilaahayoow- 'Oh Allah' -Oh my Lord

Indho deeraleey- big beautiful eyes on a woman

In sha Allah- If Allah wills it

Jilbaab- Islamic hijab that flows past knees (commonly worn by Somali women)

Jabaati - Flatbread

Jinn- Evil spirits/devils

Kaale- Come here

Khat- Plant based drug found in Somalia and parts of the Middle East

Kitaab- Book/Quran

Kufi- Muslim skullcap

Laaduu- Somali board game

Macaan- sweet

Mahadsanid- Thank you

Malawax- Somali styled crepe

Maraq- Somali styled broth/stew

Ma sha Allah- As Allah willed it (said when one sees something good, pleasing)

Masjid- Mosque

Maxaa rabtay- What did you want?

Maxaa kugu dhacay- What's wrong with you?

Maya- No

Miskiin- Innocent person

Miyaa- is that so?

Moos- Bananas

Musxaf- Copy of the quran

Naa kaalay- 'Come here, girl!'

Nasiib keyga- 'my luck'

Naayaa – Term for girl/woman (sometimes viewed as derogatory)

Oday- Old man

Qalanjo- term for tall, beautiful light skinned woman

Quran- Islamic holy book

Quruxley.- beautiful woman or girl

Rag- Man, or real man

Raali ahow – forgive me

Ramadan- Islamic holy month/ fasting

Reerka se yihiin- 'How's the family doing?'

Se layahay- 'How are you/how are you all?'

Shidni- Spicy green sauce

Sidaan isku dhaan- Do/act better than you are

Sidee tahay?- How are you?

Soo dhaaf- come inside/come in/ *Soo orod* – Hurry here

Sujood- bowing done in prayer (on the floor)

Surah Fatiha- opening chapter of the Holy Quran

Tima Hindi- Indian styled hair

Thobe- Islamic robe worn by men

Tusbaax- Islamic prayer beads

War- Boy/You boy

Wa alaykum assalam- And peace upon you (Islamic greeting)

Wallahi- 'I swear to God'/used frequently by Somali

Wanaagsan- Good/well

Xaliimo- Pronounced Halima-a name used for Somali women as a whole (sometimes in a derogatory fashion)

Xalwo- Sweet delicacy eaten by Somalis

Xamar- Capital of Somalia (Mogadishu)

Xaasidat- An expression meaning, "jealous girl or woman' (can be used playfully or in jest)

Acknowledgments

First and foremost I would like to thank Allah for giving me the chance at life and granting me the opportunity to write this book. Writing a book is a long and challenging battle, but with a little fight and putting your trust in Him, all hope is not lost.

Thank you to my parents for bringing me into this world, and making the journey to America so I could make my dream a reality. Thank you Hooyo for believing and supporting me. I owe you for all that you have sacrificed for me in your life. A big thank you to my family for all your love, help, and advice along the way.

Special thanks to my beautiful sisters, especially Faisa, Anisa, and Fartoon. They have always been my friends and supporters since day one. I don't think this book would have been at all possible without their love and guidance. Thank you Anisa for all that you've done and continue to do for me in my life. You have been one of the greatest driving forces for me to pursue this dream of mine. I am eternally grateful for all your hard work and encouragement. Love you big sis.

Major thanks to my best friend and younger sister Fartoon. Thank you for being the beautiful, hilarious, and kind hearted human you are. Along with Anisa she's been my editor, comedic relief, snack provider, and biggest source of support. Love you with all my heart man.

Thank you to Duraan, the other half of Sahal Solutions. For his time and dedication in creating my website and book cover.

I'd like to thank my good friend Hodan Moalin for instilling hope and motivation in me to write when I needed it most. She has shown me tremendous support and love along this journey, and pushed me to make this goal of mine a reality.

Thank you to my close friend Hafiza for supporting my writing, and pushing me to seek publication. She has been an amazing help throughout.

Much love to all of the friends that I made over the years and the halaqa crew. You know who you are. Thank you so much for all your constant love, support, and motivation.

Thank you to San Diego based storytelling organization *So Say We All* for helping me find my voice; assuring me this in fact something I love to do. Thank you to the friends who were there to support my performance. You guys rock.

Big thanks to all my readers from my personal blog and For Somali Gabdho for supporting my work over the years, and supporting me in my earlier writings. Ya'll are amazing.

Last but not least thank you dear reader for placing your confidence in me as a writer and reading something that has been such a long time coming. This book is dedicated to all my Somali people living in and outside of the Diaspora. Our stories mean something and our future is ever bright. All the love to you all.

About the Author

Halima Hagi-Mohamed was born in Nairobi, Kenya to Somali parents. She was raised in Fresno, California and is the second youngest of nine children. Hagi-Mohamed has been writing since the young age of twelve. She got her start by writing on popular story sharing website *Wattpad*, and later ventured into writing fictional stories about life in the Somali Diaspora. In 2010 she won the online Pen Writing Competition, placing first in her division. A year later she created, "For Somali Gabdho" alongside younger sister Fartoon, publishing short stories on *Facebook* to a growing audience of a thousand Somali women. In her free time she likes to read fiction, write stories, blog, and watch foreign movies. She currently resides with her family in San, Diego, California. "Amilah" is her first book.

To stay up to date with Amilah and any future writings, visit:

halimawrites.com

Made in the USA
San Bernardino, CA
15 January 2018